THE
DARK
REVEAL

CHURCH OF THE SEER

THE DARK REVEAL

KENYA FOUCH

BOOKLOGIX
Alpharetta, GA

ISBN: 978-1-6653-0547-1 - Paperback
eISBN: 978-1-6653-0548-8 - ePub

Library of Congress Control Number: 2023900578

☺This paper meets the requirements of ANSI/NISO Z39.48-1992
(Permanence of Paper)

011722

For Mama

① 1

SETTLING IN

MARCH 24, 2044

U kweli took a deep breath. It was a slow breath to minimize the effect on the air pressure. Slow in through the nose. Slow out through the nose. He couldn't risk opening his mouth.

Squatting with his back against the north exterior wall, Ukweli kept his chin high. His left arm reached across to his breastplate. He could feel the engraved insignia of the Church of the Seer on his armor. His right arm hung straight down as his hand rested on his firearm. Most agents preferred the newest models but the Glock G19 always made him feel authentic; like he was honoring the budding traditions of the position. He didn't want to change. Call it superstition. It's not like it mattered anyway.

Demanding focus, he looked straight ahead, pretending not to notice the large spider in the chandelier. He wondered how the creature was able to maneuver with so much dust clinging to the fixture. He didn't like spiders.

He slowly closed his eyes and took another breath, denying

his quickening heart rate. He thought of the cornucopia that added a festive elegance to the table one Thanksgiving. He thought it was corny, but Kiera insisted. She was right. He allowed himself to grin, as his heart rate finally began to settle.

Progress was slow today. The Company had been particularly active for six days. Rogue torqs were generally aggressive and reckless, but not today. This one had been deliberate and strategic.

Ukweli opened his eyes, admittedly to check the progress of the spider, when he felt a familiar chill against his right ear.

Movement.

With calm, quiet precision, he lowered his left hand while reaching his right hand toward the back of his neck to the beckoning handle of his uchigatana. He exploded from his crouched position to leverage the accuracy of his initial attack. As he spun around to face his target, he dropped to his knees and felt the resistance of flesh as his sword creased the air. He continued to spin as he rose to a standing position, delivering the second blow to the vulnerable soft tissue of the host's throat. Ukweli stood with his eyes closed, lifted his chin, and took a deep breath as the lifeless corpse fell at his feet, its head hanging by resilient strings of flesh that refused to concede. Then the familiar shriek as the symbiont escaped into the air like rising fumes from a gas tank. He felt guilty for the pride swelling up in his chest. This torq had been ruthless and deserved its fate, he thought, but the Company did seem to be targeting younger minds these days. The intel was right. The Company was definitely planning something.

He reached for his communicator and spoke, "It's Done."

He watched from outside as the vehicles arrived, carrying three crews for Cleanup.

"Guys, it's only one torq. One crew will do."

"Sorry, Captain. Cross said three. He doesn't want to chance the Company getting a read on us."

"I get it, but there's so much dust and debris in there. This place was deserted long ago. They've obviously shifted their underground operation to a different site."

"Orders, orders, sir."

"Carry on."

As Ukweli walked back toward the unit transport vehicle, he received an incoming call.

"Gee. Thanks, UK."

"Why the sarcasm, Jason?"

"Oh, I don't know. Cleanup draggin' another host in here in a bucket. Why you gotta be so gruesome?"

"There's plenty of remains for the software to ID."

"Barely. Maybe if you used your gun just once. And how old was this guy? Sixteen?"

"Old enough to decide to join the Reveal. And Obi-Wan was right. Guns are uncivilized."

Ukweli took a seat near the front of the transport, leaned back, and kicked his feet out before resting his head against a bag on the shelf behind him. His team preferred guns to swords but marveled at his precision and feared him just enough to keep their ideas to themselves. This was only the second full-team mission, and Ukweli wondered why the Church didn't trust him to handle it solo. Perhaps there was developing dissension, but Ukweli didn't see how that was his problem. Maybe he just didn't want to see it.

3

2

THE LEGEND
BEGINS

Kabeyesi Aseyori was born in October 1995, to cassava farmers in Nigeria. He was forced to learn Thai so he could help his father create, negotiate, and maintain trade partners on the Asian island. He was raised Catholic and was trained to believe in the ability of physical labor to positively adjust one's character. His life experience, however, drew him to the conclusion that education transcends work. "All achievements begin in the mind," he would say. While he greatly respected his father's wisdom, toughness, and work ethic, he simply had no intentions of living the life of a farmer. He loved to read and gravitated toward math and science. He found his first love in a physics book. Technically, his second love too.

Unimara Bakari was born in August 1996, to exporters in east Tanzania on the coast of the Indian Ocean. While most young Tanzanian girls are taught a trade, the merchant class is affluent in Tanga so Unimara was lovingly nudged into education and the arts. Unimara was born with a quiet confidence, but her friends were drawn to her humility. She encouraged them to call her Mara.

Her future was perfectly diagrammed so she'd eventually take over the family business. Economics, marketing, shipping, and first chair on the oboe . . . everything that she would need to manage an East African port. Her plans changed when she met her first love, football, and her second love, physics. The former would create a path to Caleb University, a faith-based institution within walking distance of the new, state-of-the-art football training facility in Lagos. Plus, the campus was relatively new, so the science labs were up to date. The latter would merge her path with her future spouse, via the 2016 African Physics Bowl, where her team from Caleb narrowly defeated Kabeyesi's team from Lagos University thanks to Mara's unusual affection for Quantum Physics.

The two bitter rivals fell in love and united over the aggregate of sports and science. Kabeyesi developed a passion for basketball after watching Team USA in the 2008 Olympics. His friends even started calling him "Kobe" after he became a superfan of the superstar following the Beijing games. Mara's dreams of being an Olympian fell short due to a knee injury, but she continued to follow the sport and became a fan of the English Premier League's Aston Villa upon their signing of Tanzanian national Mbwana Samatta.

Kobe and Mara spent their time together watching the Lakers or Aston Villa and arguing about the merits of string theory versus loop quantum gravity. A unified theory indeed.

By the time their first child, Ukweli, was born, Kobe and

Mara were married and employed in the physics department at LU. They purchased a home on Lagos Island. Not that either cared, but both understood the importance of image in Lagos high society. The schools were good and the neighborhood was safe. Relatively.

Ukweli Rahisi Aseyori was born on January 4, 2020, at St. Nicholas Hospital on Lagos Island. Mara was a very protective and untrusting mother and it only served to heighten her resolve that Ukweli was born in the bantling stages of the Covid-19 pandemic.

Ukweli was raised to be tough and was influenced by his grandfather's notion of hypermasculinity—but make no mistake, he was a mama's boy. He grew up like most of the other kids on the island, living in the suburbs and attending private schools with a busy schedule and high expectations.

Ukweli excelled at most things. He took his first steps at six months and spoke in full sentences before his first birthday. The teachers at the Jolas School considered him a marvel, primarily because he could color inside the lines. He was ahead of the curve by every measure, both physically and mentally.

Ukweli showed great promise in his physical education classes, enough to catch the eye of the youth scouts for the Super Eagles who requested that his training be moved to their facility in the city. He learned languages easily and spoke fluently in Yoruba and English. Mara insisted on his Swahili name so that someday he might be driven to take a deeper dive into Tanzanian culture.

While Ukweli recognized the ease with which he learned things that seemed difficult for his peers, he was equally bored by most of what school had to offer. The only thing that really moved Ukweli's young mind was winning. He loved to compete. He loved to win. He loved to watch his peers, even his friends, agonize over their certain defeat. He loved to beat people at stuff, all kinds of stuff. Football. Squash. Kendo. Jujutsu. Debate. Video games. Card games. Board games.

Ukweli was the apple of his mother's eye. He made his father proud. He was poised and strong. He was in control. He lived to be showered with the love of his mama and papa. He was an only child and his lack of social skills reflected it. He had lots of friends because his peers *wanted* to be friends with him. He never initiated a friendship. He enjoyed the freedom that came with being an only child.

Until three years later, when he wasn't anymore.

"Ukweli, come here and show your sister some attention. She needs to get to know you."

"She can't do anything but make weird noises and smells."

"Not now, but one day soon, she will be able to do things."

"I'll get to know her then."

"If you don't help her now, she may not ever get good at things."

"So?"

"She is your sister. If she is not good at things people may think you're not good at things either."

"No one will ever think that. They will see me being good at things."

"Are you really willing to take that risk?"

Mothers can be very persuasive. Ukweli would have to be much more careful with his words in future debates with Mama. Nevertheless, Uzuri Kitendo Aseyori would become a fixture at Ukweli's side. He would teach her what she needed to know to someday be an adequate representative for the family. First and foremost, she needed to learn pool-party etiquette.

"You're going to learn to swim today."

"I don't know how to swim."

"I know. That's why I said that you're going to learn today."

"Did Papa say I have to learn today?"

"No. But I'm going to teach you."

"How can you teach me? You're little too."

"I'm seven and that's old enough to know you need to be swimming. You'll be five soon, and people will start to invite you to pool parties."

"None of my friends in school can swim."

"Then they can embarrass their own brothers."

"What if I swim at parties but my friends don't swim?"

"Then you win."

Uzuri did eventually become an excellent swimmer. She would also learn that Ukweli was right about pool parties. Her friends all hated her with a white-hot jealousy, because when she was invited to pool parties, her friends would sit on the side of the pool or wade in the shallows while Uzuri would immediately head for the deeper water. The host's mom would inevitably rush to the edge of the pool, filled with concern, only to find Uzuri doing deep water laps.

Samantha from school once omitted Uzuri from her pool-party invite list and began spreading negative gossip. She called Uzuri a tomboy and said she "didn't need any stinky fish in her pool." Uzuri asked Samantha "if she needed any peanut butter for her jelly" and became a playground legend. The other girls decided they should also learn how to swim.

Uzuri was a trendsetter. Her opinion mattered. The little boys at school all wanted to be around her but because she didn't want to be around them, they hated her. The little girls at the school all wanted her to like them, but she didn't like them and they hated her too. She liked that they all hated her, and that, given complicated adolescent protocols, made her the most popular girl in the school.

Uzuri was prettier than the other girls and a better swimmer than the boys. She stood out on the pitch and was made to play in a higher age range before, eventually, being granted her request to play with the boys. She found no satisfaction in scoring goals against girls.

Uzuri was an excellent student, and her teachers would always send notes home to her parents like "joy to teach" and "very bright." Uzuri didn't care about the notes, but she knew they made Mama and Papa happy. She did, however, care about her grades, and would often argue with a teacher who gave her anything less than an A+, one hundred, or E. When Mrs. Ridgway sent a note home saying, "Uzuri was sassy today"—because Uzuri asked her if she needed any peanut butter for her jelly—she decided she would take any necessary steps in the future to keep her instructors on her side. She also decided to retire the "peanut butter for your jelly" response. You don't do the same gag twice.

When she was seven, Uzuri was invited to her first boygirl pool party. She was excited because this was her first time attending a party with Ukweli. He stood to the side and watched with pride as Uzuri dominated all competition in the swim races. Ukweli knew that his friends liked his little sister, and he knew they wouldn't dare speak a word to her while he was there. Uzuri also knew Ukweli's friends liked her, and that they wouldn't dare speak a word to her while her big brother was there. They were both happy about this.

Uzuri got out of the pool, grabbed her towel and a cup of

punch, and made her way to the corner where Ukweli was now entertaining Samantha from school. She noticed that Ukweli was moving awkwardly, like a robot, and talking in an unusually low register. She walked over and grabbed her big brother by the arm.

"Excuse me, Sam, but I need to talk with Kweli for a second."

"What's good, Zuri?" Ukweli asked as he was being dragged away.

"You like Samantha from school?" she forcefully whispered.

"Huh? We were just talking."

"Yeah, looking crazy and trying to sound like a grown man."

"Quit tripping. I'm just here to enjoy the party. I can't help who comes over to talk to me."

"Listen, you're not going to embarrass me at this party."

"I'm sure that I don't know what you're talking about."

"Think of something funny and be cool."

"Thanks for the unnecessary advice." Only it was necessary advice. It was advice that he would take with him into battle and his future attempts at courting.

He had created a monster in Uzuri and he was so proud. They were inseparable. They would go to parties together and train for football season together. They spent a lot of time with each other because Mama and Papa were almost always in the lab. Once Mara fully convinced Kobe of the value of quantum physics, they made a breakthrough together that changed the world and their family's fortune.

"For their use of nanotechnology to minimize the effects of quantum tunneling in transistors, the 2030 Nobel Prize in Physics is awarded to Drs. Kabeyesi and Unimara Aseyori of Nigeria."

The words of Queen Victoria of Sweden rang loud and clear in the Stockholm Concert Hall that December. Kobe and Mara elegantly ascended the short stairs to the main stage to accept their award and present their lectures.

Mara spoke briefly about her love for her husband and children and how they inspired her every day to pursue a better world for them. She spoke of her love for Christ and his principles that influenced her daily decisions. She spoke about Hope, and how she longed for Unity. She was beautiful and smart and Uzuri cried. Ukweli was very proud of her but refused to show that kind of emotion.

Kobe quickly mentioned his family but focused his lecture on the scientific impact of the discovery. He spoke of the new world that could exist because of the computing power allowed by eliminating quantum tunneling. He conveyed his excitement concerning improvements in health care with quicker and more accurate diagnoses. He lectured about benefits in economics as transferring funds would be more secure, untraceable, and faster, even internationally. He spoke of satellites that could go farther and see more, and technology that could help lessen the devastating effects of global warming. Depending on your perspective, it was a speech full of promise and hope or a speech full of corruption and greed.

3

THINGS ARE CHANGING

K obe and Mara had grown in international fame seem-
ingly overnight. The now-Nobel laureates were rock-
stars in their field and were the highest-paid employees at
Lagos University. They received additional awards, and additional funding, from the city of Lagos, the nation of
Nigeria, the Scientific Council of Tanzania, the World
Health Organization, and the CDC, and they were asked to
present in places like Boston, Sydney, and London. Sometimes, Ukweli and Uzuri tagged along. Most of the time
they didn't.

Ukweli was a mature eleven years old, practically an
adult, and the neighborhood was safe, so Ukweli and Uzuri
just stayed home and helped raise each other. Ukweli
helped Uzuri with her schoolwork and Uzuri helped
Ukweli be less awkward. Kobe and Mara didn't insist that
the children attend mass when they were out of town (Kobe
didn't really want to go himself), but Mara did expect them

to work through their Bible study materials and she would question them on video chat during her flights. Mara wanted her children to have something that resembled a traditional upbringing, and she believed exposure to biblical principles would help fill in the gaps. With how often she and her husband were on the road and away from their children, she was counting on it. Kobe and Mara traveled throughout the spring and into the summer that year.

In July 2031, the family began to host dignitaries for brunch and dinner events. Heads of state from nations all over Africa and Europe trekked to Lagos Island to have an audience with the brightest minds in the world at the time. Kobe and Mara entertained house guests every weekend through July and August. Visitors were treated with daring tales of discovery that Kobe would share, while Mara served as a gracious hostess. The couple provided cigars and whiskey for the men, and the ladies if they so desired, along with mimosas or vintage wine. The men eventually retreated to Kobe's study and the women transitioned to Mara's nook on the lagoon. There was lots of laughter and handshakes and Bach and caviar and enough pretentiousness to go around.

Even when Kobe and Mara were home, somehow Ukweli and Uzuri ended up entertaining each other. Ukweli enjoyed the extra free time. Uzuri resented the fact that she wasn't allowed to participate in the salons.

Kobe once came out of the study to find Uzuri kneeling on the other side of the door. He introduced her as Nigeria's next great scholar and footballer and the guests acted impressed. When the visitors had gone, Uzuri asked Kobe what his meetings were about and he responded, "We're improving on God's good work." Uzuri didn't know what that meant, but she was proud of her father and trusted him implicitly. He was a good man.

In August, Kobe and Mara hosted a delegation from the United States. The American president was not in attendance but the vice president and several representatives of the cabinet and congress—perhaps a dozen—made the trans-Atlantic flight. The meal chosen by the caterer was described as Carolina-style barbecue, with spicy shredded pork shoulder and coleslaw (neither Kobe nor Mara ate pork) and two kegs of bronze lager. The Americans were loud and obnoxious, right on par with their dubious reputation. They told jokes that made Mara cringe and spoke openly about their disdain for their political rivals back home. Their love of their guns was only surpassed by their love for their flag. Ukweli was surprised to hear one of the Americans quote his father when he patted Ukweli on the head after returning from the restroom (his hands were moist but did not smell like soap) and said, "Son, you should be very proud of your papa. He's improving on God's good work." Those words sounded curious coming from his father's mouth and quite ridiculous and offensive spoken by this inebriated, crude character.

As the group, including the two American females, made their way to Kobe's study, their loud and boisterous, celebratory tones took an aggressive turn. There was some shouting and two of the American men had to be separated once. As it were, the argument concerned two American baseball teams. They also took sports very seriously there, evidently. When the group finally emerged from the closed doors of the study after two hours, twice as long as the other meetings, things seemed to have calmed and there was a sense of anticipation. Everyone was nervous but eager. Anxious but hopeful.

Ukweli was uncomfortable because his father usually spoke in very negative connotations about these types of people. He told Ukweli that Americans were fat and arrogant and, though they had abundant resources, they were not to be trusted. Uzuri hugged Mama's shoulder because she was noticeably distressed as she sat at the dining room table. Ukweli wondered what changed his father's mind about their visitors from the west. The children knew that things were changing and that something was coming.

4

THE
MANIFESTATION

President Vincent Rhett sat in the chair at his desk in the oval office with his back turned to his guests, reclining as he faced the window. Standing next to the desk was his chief of staff, Trevor Boseman, and lead White House counsel, Ben Clarke. Seated on the couches were members of the religious community, representatives from the Southern Baptist Convention, United Methodist Church, Buddhist Churches of America, the United Synagogue, the Muslim American Society, and the Conference of Bishops. Each sat quietly, eagerly awaiting the arrival of the president's guest of honor. The business community had already been informed and was on board. While they were skeptical as to whether or not President Rhett could live up to his promises, they were willing to wait it out at the mere possibilities.

"How much longer did they say it was going to be?"

"Not long now, Mr. President. The motorcade is already on the move."

"So he's actually here. We're actually doing this."

"What do you mean, sir?"

"I mean that I've never believed in all of this until now. I grew up in a semi-religious household, and I've always believed in some form of a higher power, but I never knew there was more to it than the Ten Commandments, really. Now, I wouldn't be surprised to see an actual wizard walk through those doors."

"His presentation was quite convincing, sir. He showed us things that even our scientific community never experienced before. Things will never be the same after today."

"Yeah, so I've heard."

After another three awkwardly quiet minutes, the silence was abruptly broken by the hidden door of the oval office being clumsily flung open and two agents in suits and sunglasses forcefully entered, followed by a small man in a vest. Boseman walked over to the man and put his right hand on his back while using his left hand to guide him toward the vacant chair in front of the president's desk.

"Mr. President, I would like you to meet Dr. Kabeyesi Aseyori."

OCTOBER 16, 2031

President Rhett stood behind the presidential podium in the White House rose garden. It was a beautiful October morning, and the weather was clear and crisp. He took a deep breath and allowed a sun ray to warm his face before he addressed the nation. With members of the business and religious communities standing behind him, and Dr. Kobe Aseyori standing beside him, President Rhett began:

"My fellow American citizens and citizens of the world, I am so honored and excited to share this paradigm-shifting revelation with you today. After meeting with Dr. Aseyori and my friends from the commerce and religious communities all over our awesome country, it is my great pleasure to usher our nation, and indeed the entire globe, into a new era of technology sharing. Dr. Aseyori of Nigeria and his beautiful wife, Unimara, have unlocked the secrets of new dimensions in time and space to reveal to us technologies unlike anything our planet has seen before. With these new developments, we will accomplish things that were not even possible in our dreams. Every system: healthcare, computing, economics, and religion will experience a shove into the future that, dare I say, represents an improvement on God's good work. We found the key to unlocking the truth of prosperity and wellness and we're pushing our chips to the middle of the table. We're all in with the Company and we're fervently moving forward."

There is a pause for boisterous, participatory applause . . .

"I would like to introduce, to everyone, Dr. Kabeyesi Aseyori of Nigeria."

Ukweli watched on the news, as his father explained to the world how Unimara had visions of the quantum world since she was in grade school and began to have dreams and hear voices describing quantum technology during her college years. When they met, he explained, he was stunned at her understanding of quantum physics but, as they grew closer, she reluctantly revealed to him that she often received information from the voices. Once they were married, the "voices" began to appear as shapes or shadows and claimed to be from other dimensions or distant planets. They would often visit the couple during their collaborative work time and eventually advised them of the nanotech solution to quantum tunneling for which they received the Nobel Prize. When a reporter stood up and asked what the mysterious beings wanted in return for their generous contributions, Kobe responded, "They just want to help us improve on God's good work. After all, isn't that exactly what God ordered us to do?"

A reporter raised his hand but did not wait to be acknowledged.

"Dr. Aseyori, Billy Pate. How do we contact these beings, or do we just wait for them to contact you or your wife?"

"That's the best news, Billy. These beings have been on our planet for thousands of years and they're all around us. They're here right now. You just only need ears that are willing to hear."

"So, I can hear from these beings on my own?"

"Yes, sir, you can. Anyone can. You only need to clear your mind and open your heart and you too can help us improve on God's good work."

"Okay, everyone, thank you for coming out today. We will continue to keep you informed of any new developments. Please be safe traveling." The chief counsel released the microphone and walked behind the president and Kobe as reporters continued to shout questions.

"Is this a new world religion?"

"Why are the members of the religious community here for the announcement?"

"What is Dr. Aseyori's role in our government?"

"There's no such thing as a free lunch!"

Kobe returned home to a chaotic scene at the Lagos Airport. There were protesters and counter-protesters striped along the loading area. Kobe and Mara now required security teams when they traveled and their home on Lagos Island was constantly under surveillance. The protesters weren't violent, but they were noisy and annoying. There were even different cults forming; some in honor of Kobe, some for Mara, and some for the otherworldly beings that make up the Company. Some groups built statues or shrines. Others wrote poems and sang songs.

In the days following Kobe's announcement in Washington, twelve more heads-of-state of world governments released statements concerning their meetings with the Aseyori family and confirmed their support for the Company. (Kobe described his encounters with the beings as "having company.") More and more people were beginning to report detailed encounters with the strange visitors. Some of the accounts described out-of-body experiences to the far edges of space, and others reported learning details about some previously unknown gadget or hearing a song or poem in an unidentified language. However, some encounters were darker in nature, reporting that the shadows urged or demanded they commit crimes or violence.

OCTOBER 30, 2031

Two weeks after President Rhett stood in the rose garden with Dr. Aseyori, he received a phone call from the Vatican. He had been eagerly awaiting information from Pope Gregory as the Conference of Bishops assured him that the Holy See would be supportive of the drastic changes. The pope apologized for the delayed contact but explained that the subject matter was obviously very sensitive and required a great deal of deliberation. The pope elucidated that he understood the need for open and vocal support from the religious community for such a delicate maneuver but that he was having trouble accepting the paramount request from our visitors.

"Your holiness, I can understand your trepidation. I have moved cautiously through this entire process and the Company has exceeded my expectations at each and every junction. We have seen our GDP rise six percent in two weeks since the announcement. Even our ability to track such things wouldn't have been possible before they arrived. Prices are down and wages are up. We have done what they have asked of us, and they have rewarded us one hundred times over. Every investment has produced a positive return. Every agreement has been beneficial. I know our latest request is extremely difficult, but I think we can admit that far too many of the wars fought on our planet have been over religious differences. True religious freedom is a myth. Just think of the peace that we can broker with a single world religion. Once we have rid ourselves of the divisiveness of the planet's many different holy books, the Company will be free to aid our establishment of a single religion with you, the most beloved and respected spiritual leader in the world, as the head of the organization."

After a long pause, the voice on the other end of the phone responded with a heavy, old-world Italian accent, "You're asking me to disavow the Holy Bible."

"Yes, sir. Well, the Company is asking you. The world is asking you. They manifest tomorrow and they would like your support."

"I hope you understand that I simply cannot. *Hoc est vere in revelare tenebris.*"

"I'm sorry to hear that. Perhaps we can be more convincing in the future."

OCTOBER 31, 2031

It was conceivably a great coincidence, or none whatsoever, that the Manifestation was executed on a Halloween Friday. President Rhett, with the White House lawn full of children dressed as ghosts, goblins, superheroes, princesses, and the like, sat behind his desk in the oval office with a single empty chair beside him. There was no staff present, only a lone cameraman with a single spotlight in an otherwise dark room. President Rhett adjusted his tie, cleared his throat, and nervously spoke as he was instructed, "Welcome to the Manifestation."

A figure slowly began to take shape in the space above the empty chair next to the president. It initially began as a transparent blue gel, like looking into a clear bottle of aloe vera. As the form began to define, the gel slowly, but deliberately, took the shape of a woman. A beautiful blond woman with a thick Texas accent said, "Hey y'all."

President Rhett sat quietly, if not in stunned silence, and observed the figure in the chair beside him. He struggled to fix his face, remembering that he was in a live worldwide broadcast. The woman was shockingly beautiful with piercing blue eyes and a pearly white smile. She looked to be in her twenties but spoke with the reassurance of a southern grandmother.

"I'm so pleased that President Rhett has invited me to Washington. It's my first time here and it's such a lovely place. My name is Annabelle Jefferson, but y'all can just call me Ann. I'm super duper excited to be here representing my friends and family and helping y'all improve on God's good work. You know, when the good lord made all of heaven and earth and all the creatures big and small, he stepped back and said that it was good. While we do appreciate the contributions of the almighty God, what if we want *great*? Well, my friends and family and I are doing just that. We're here—right here on planet Earth—to improve on God's good work. It's really what God wants us to do. We're here to make it great!"

Ann rose out of her seat and grabbed President Rhett's hand, prompting him to stand. She lifted her hands, and his, above her head, and shouted, "Make it great!" on rhythm until Rhett was obligated to join. Suddenly, the curtains flew open and an ensemble orchestra appeared in the room playing the '80s relief aid song, "We Are The World," while a fireworks simulation ignited inside the office creating an explosion of sound and light.

President Rhett continued to stand with his mouth open. Ann returned to her seat and the orchestra softly, but with great intensity, began to play "Eye of the Tiger."

"Every civilization that ever made the step from good to great had one thing in common—unity. We're here so that you can enjoy the freedom that comes with knowing your truth. Absolutes are the human constructs that bind you in slavery. Absolutes incubate and breed corruption. We're going to make the most significant changes in the history of this good world, but it starts with you. It starts with you putting aside your petty differences and joining your duly elected officials around the world, with the support of your community leaders and your religious representatives, in the complete destruction of all the hateful, divisive so-called holy books. We know these books haven't done anything in your short history but start trouble, introduce unrealistic and unsupported expectations, and bring strife. They highlight your differences and force you to focus on what divides you. Well, that ends today! We're all coming together—and when I say all, I mean all. Every nation in all parts of the world, we're all coming together to ban these aggressive and violent texts so that we can move into a world of peace and love together. With our technology and your love and unity, we will make this world great!"

The orchestra seamlessly transitioned to "We Didn't Start the Fire."

"Go out and grab every Bible, Torah, and Talmud. Collect the Koran and the Hadith. The Vedas, the Gita, and the Tao.

Take them to the nearest fire and toss them in. Nothing will stand in the way of our great love! We will forever remember this moment as the night we reclaimed our peace and stood together as one great world! One unity. One world. One heart. One love!"

The world experienced a complete and thorough literary expurgation.

Uncontrolled riots commenced on every corner of the globe. Every bookstore and library. Personal homes and commercial buildings. Every book in every room in every building became a target for Torqueo Anima. That's what the Vatican called them. It wasn't long before someone said "torqs" and the name stuck. The torqs in most places participated in a celebratory riot that destroyed books and property. The torqs that attacked the Vatican that night were far more sinister, and actually killed two people who were defending the archives.

Following Ann Jefferson's motivational speech, the Company rose up by the millions to inhabit willing hosts all over the planet. The first night alone, Halloween night, the first night of the Manifestation, torqs did an estimated eight hundred billion dollars worth of damage, including catastrophic destruction at the Vatican, the Dome of the Rock, and the Western Wall. Large churches in America were targeted in Atlanta, Houston, New York, Los Angeles, and Chicago. And then, as quickly as it all started, it all ended— precisely at eleven p.m. in Atlanta. Eleven a.m. in Hong Kong. Four a.m. in Lagos.

5

THE AFTERMATH

K obe sat in front of his computer and listened. He woke up during the night when all the commotions started, but his house, his wife, and his children had never been in any real danger. In fact, no torqs came to their house during the Manifestation. Kobe made a cup of coffee, a Kaldi premiere roast, and muted his microphone. He would certainly be asked to address the group today. While dignitaries and heads of state went back and forth concerning the results of the Manifestation, Kobe browsed the internet to look at photos of the global damage. "Not as bad as I thought, honestly," he whispered to himself as he shrugged his shoulders. He took another warm sip as President Rhett began to address the video conference.

"Ladies and gentlemen, please. . . . The Manifestation was an enormous success. We just endured a worldwide riot with fewer than five casualties. It's over and everyone is home. The planet is waking to a new reality. We can handle this! Everything is right on schedule. I'm gonna bring in

Dr. Aseyori and he can answer your questions. We'll hear from Ann tomorrow. Doctor?"

Kobe unmuted his microphone. "Thank you, President Rhett. I've been checking my email this morning and I seem to be getting the same three or four questions from everyone, so I'll address those. Let's deal with the bad news first. We have allowed the Vatican to get out in front of us and their expressions for our initiatives are beginning to stick. It hasn't changed any outcomes yet, but we really want the world to refer to our great, future momentum as the Movement—not the Dark Reveal as I've been seeing on news tickers this morning. Also, the media is referring to inhabited hosts as torqs. Most people won't know what that means but we really must continue to stress that hosts are inhabited voluntarily and that at no time has the Company fully inhabited a host against their will. The Company reserves the right to influence minds even if they don't inhabit the full machine. Now, the good news. We will all make a significant sum once we release our reconstruction plans. Our new building materials and recycling plants will make cleanup move quickly so that the population can return to a sense of normalcy. After Ann's announcement tomorrow morning, we will see a real shift in this fight for the hearts and minds of our planet. Congratulations, and welcome to the Great World!"

Mara sat on the edge of the bed with her face in her hands. She swiped down, feeling for sleep crust on the way. She opened her eyes just in time to see Ukweli come into the room, his steps soft and deliberate.

"Good morning, Mama."

"Good morning, sweetie. Were you able to sleep?"

"Yes. I left my tv on," Ukweli said as he climbed onto the bed and plopped on a pillow.

"I hope you haven't been watching the news. Things have really gotten pretty crazy."

"Is Papa okay?"

"I'm not sure . . . of course. He's very busy, but he's strong."

"Are you okay?"

"Hmmm . . . how about waffles for breakfast? Go wash your hands."

Mama energetically bounced off the bed and with two claps summoned Ukweli to follow her downstairs. No need to wake Uzuri. She could smell waffles from kilometers away.

As Ukweli approached the bottom few stairs, he could hear Mama and Papa engaged in a discussion that seemed too intense for waffles.

"Not this morning, Kobe. I just want to enjoy breakfast with the piglets and maybe catch up on some shows. I want to be accomplishment free for one day please."

"Mara, I know that these have been stressful times for you. I apologize that I haven't been able to shield you from all of this like I told you I would. It doesn't matter how I try, the Company has insisted on your involvement. They've been concerned about you. They're starting to question your resolve, but I've constantly assured them that you're just as committed as you were on day one. Am I right?"

Mara's ice-cold glance told Kobe that he should give her a few minutes.

Mara had never been comfortable with the Company. Even from the very first days when they would whisper test answers into her ear, or when everyone at the African Physics Bowl was completely shocked by her correct answer in the bonus round, Mara suspected they had an agenda. Mara desperately wanted to believe that the Company desired to make the world better, and she was all for an improved world to hand off to her kids. Their collaboration with the visitors, however, seemed to be moving in a different direction since the Nobel presentation. The collective effort that had been centered around the movement from good to great was slowly starting to feel like the opening act for a much more sinister plot. She never thought she would live to see a single world religion, much less one that would take the place of the others following a single event on a single night. She certainly never thought she would see Muslims burning the Koran or southern gentlemen standing around a Bible-fueled bonfire.

"What can I do to ease your mind about this?"

"Nothing, Kobe. I just don't think that you've considered all the possibilities."

"We've been over this again and again. It's under control. I don't know what else you want me to say."

"There's no way that you or the Company have prepared for resistance. This planet may be new and small, but it's full of very stubborn people. Have you even heard from the Vatican?"

"I'm sure Gregory will come around. If not, Ann has already talked to Rhett about contingencies."

"Ann . . ." she said as she rolled her eyes. She flipped the waffle iron to start the clock. "Ann is grossly underestimating the will of humans to fight anything they don't understand. They *will* form a resistance and right now . . ." She hesitated and then released a stressed sigh. "I just don't trust them. They keep changing the rules and they're obviously motivated by a much higher goal than improving on God's good world. They said that the single world religion was the endgame to peace, to assist in the sharing of technology. It is obvious, now, that it's just the beginning of some other objective and I'm pretty sure we're not going to like where the road ends."

"Mara, when this is all over, regardless of how it ends, we're going to be the ones on top."

"Maybe. But who cares if you own one hundred percent of nothing?"

Ukweli jumped down to the floor from the bottom step and quickly rushed over to the waffle iron. It had beeped ten times by now and was starting to smoke. He turned it over, separated the two halves, and started to scrape off the crusty remains of the overcooked try. He liked a good crispy waffle, but this was burnt beyond saving. He quickly discarded the first waffle, gave the iron a warm blanket of butter-flavored anti-stick spray, and layered the grill with a fresh coating of sweet batter. Mama always added cinnamon and brown sugar to the waffle batter to make it extra sweet and even more delicious. Mama's waffles had a good, sweet taste even without syrup, but he always added it and butter anyway. They didn't get to eat sugary breakfast foods like waffles very often, so Ukweli was fully prepared to take advantage of the opportunity.

As he flipped the iron, he heard Uzuri coming down the last few stairs and around the corner.

"Why are you down here burning up innocent waffles?"

"Mama got distracted."

"Yeah, she's been a space cadet lately. I've never seen her worry this much in my life."

"She was tapping her fingers on the table yesterday and it sounded like one of Cameron's old beats. I started rapping. She stopped and threw a napkin at me and told me I needed to take my life more seriously. Then she got up and hugged me. She could tell that I was a little freaked out. Waffle's up."

There were very few things in life that couldn't be cleared up by a good, sweet, crispy waffle. Mama and Papa continued to whisper-argue, while Ukweli and Uzuri enjoyed their breakfast in front of the television. Every station was talking about the Dark Reveal last night. That was, except for one, Complete Sports Nigeria. Football highlights and crispy waffles might be the perfect combination.

The siblings knew their parents were on edge. They knew something was coming. They didn't know what it was, but they figured it would happen soon. All the more reason to enjoy their waffles while they could. Honestly, though, if something really bad was coming, maybe that meant they would get waffles more often. You know . . . silver linings.

6

MORE THINGS CHANGE FOREVER

U zuri struggled to fall asleep. She tossed and turned. She tried reading the most boring thing she had, one of Mama's physics books. She stared at the ceiling and counted the glow-in-the-dark star stickers. She counted antelopes. She even turned the tv to a cricket match. Nothing worked. She heard in a movie that warm milk could help you sleep so she headed downstairs to give it a shot. She simply couldn't stop her mind from racing. She was so worried about Mama.

As she quietly descended the stairs, she heard voices. Her first thought was how ridiculous it was that Mama and Papa could still be in the kitchen, arguing at one a.m. *Just let it go already*, she thought to herself, as she slowly rounded the corner at the bottom of the stairs. She held up her head to look at the table in the breakfast nook and was shocked

31

to see that Papa wasn't talking to Mama. It was Ann—the lady from the tv.

"Sweetie, wow, I'm so sorry. Have we interrupted your sleep?"

"No . . . I'm sorry, Papa. I haven't been able to get to sleep at all. My mind is racing. I was gonna try some warm milk."

Uzuri could see that her father seemed nervous, almost fearful. It made her uncomfortable but strengthened her resolve.

"Do you guys want some milk?" She tilted her head to the side as she pointed toward the fridge.

"No . . . thank you. Ahh, Uzuri, do you remember Ann?"

"No. I saw her on tv but I never met her. Hi," Uzuri spoke from behind the opened refrigerator door.

"Hello, darling. I sincerely apologize for disturbing your rest."

Uzuri sensed sarcasm but let it go.

"It wasn't you."

Uzuri grabbed the milk carton and set it on the counter then grabbed a small glass from the cabinet. The two adults sat silently in the nook while she moved around the kitchen. Uzuri poured a few ounces of milk, replaced the cap, and returned the milk to its place in the fridge. As she reached around to put the glass into the microwave, she noticed movement out of the corner of her eye.

She quickly turned her head toward the movement to see two men standing at the base of the stairs. It was as if they had been there the whole time. Uzuri screamed as she dropped the glass and took three steps back as it shattered on the floor. The men were very large and dressed in all black; t-shirts, jeans, and sneakers. They just stood there and looked around as if they were as surprised as she was they were there.

Kobe stood up. Ann remained seated.

"Why have you come into my home?"

"Where is it?" The first man asked as they both sauntered around the large island in the kitchen toward the nook, away from Uzuri.

"Where is what?" Kobe responded.

"Where is she?" the second man asked.

"Where is who?" Uzuri reacted.

Mara, having heard Uzuri scream, came bursting out of the bedroom and stopped at the top of the stairs with her right hand on the banister. She quickly surveyed the room as her eyes moved from right to left; Kobe stood, Ann sat, Uzuri was in the kitchen, near the fridge, and the two large men were now looking at her.

"Where is it?" the first man asked again, this time to Mara.

"You come into my home, where my children are, and make inquiries?"

"I won't ask again," the first man said, as he reached toward the small of his back and grabbed a black, matte pistol. He pointed it directly at her.

"Mara, please," Kobe said, as he took a step toward his wife.

"I'm not afraid of your juvenile intimidations." Mara walked down the stairs as she spoke. "Tell your rapacious boss, whoever he is, that he can bid and wait, like everyone else." She stopped on the second step from the bottom. "Get out of my home, right now."

"Wrong answer, lady."

A single shot rang out like a firecracker pop. The sound was high-pitched, clean, clear, and it stunned Kobe's ears and made him blink—frozen in place. Mara saw the flash and heard the pop and began to imagine what heaven would be like. She never felt the bullet, but she closed her eyes and started feeling her abdomen for what would surely be an entry wound. After a few seconds, she opened her eyes and took a breath; she hadn't been breathing.

She looked down and saw a circle of blood pooling on the kitchen floor. Only it wasn't hers. Uzuri lay motionless at her feet.

Kobe, returning from his momentary paralyzation, opened his eyes. Mara was on the floor, on her knees crying and holding Uzuri as she shivered. The men were gone. Ann was gone too.

"Call for help, Kobe!" The command was made in a voice that Kobe would never forget. He never heard Mara panic before, and the fear in her voice instantly made him cry.

He grabbed his phone and, after a short pause said, "Please hurry. My daughter's been shot!"

Ukweli was standing tall with the football between his feet. He looked straight ahead and smirked at the keeper, able to see the concern in his eyes. This would be the third consecutive world cup match where the Super Eagles asked him to take a penalty in the second half of a tied game. Their spread offense put so much pressure on defenses and he was the perfect midfielder, possessing impeccable passing and shooting abilities. Every one of the thirty thousand fans in Godswill Akpabio stadium knew exactly what was about to happen. He always delivered for his team and his nation.

Pop!

Ukweli was abruptly awakened from his dream by a loud noise. He couldn't tell if it was from inside or outside the house. He lay still in bed for a few seconds and listened for anything to guide his next action. He jumped out of bed and ran out of his room to the top of the staircase. He looked down the stairs and saw Mama on her knees on the floor. Papa came into the room from the front door, followed by two emergency medical personnel.

Ukweli's eyes returned to Mama and only when she let out a primal scream did he notice that she was holding a bloody body. Ukweli ran down the stairs, almost tripping on one, and stopped on the second step. Papa helped pry the body away from Mama's hands and Ukweli saw Uzuri's pale face as the medical workers began to tear her clothes away. They quickly transferred her to a gurney and whisked her toward the front door.

Papa grabbed Mama's shoulders and said, "Let's go honey." Mama slowly rose to her feet, and she and Papa briskly followed the medics out the front door. They closed the door behind them without saying a word. When the neighbors arrived six minutes later, Ukweli was standing silently in his pajamas, with his bare feet in the puddle of blood.

"Tragic news in the world of politics tonight. Uzuri Aseyori, the daughter of Drs. Kabeyesi and Unimara Aseyori, was tragically murdered during a home invasion at the family's Lagos Island estate. The Nobel laureates' daughter was described as smart, athletic, and fun-loving. She was only nine years old."

The day after the invasion, the university sent a crew to deep clean the home. They were very thorough in their efforts, especially in the kitchen, where they ripped out the hardwood and replaced it with gray ceramic. They stocked the pantry and refrigerator with food and snacks. They boxed all the clothing from Uzuri's room and placed the items into storage to await instructions from Mara.

The Aseyori family was given twenty-four-hour access to the grief counselors from the University. They did not use them.

Mara couldn't look at Ukweli without thinking of Uzuri. The family became a group of isolated individuals. They were no longer a unit. The family no longer celebrated holidays. Mara gave Ukweli $100 on his birthday each year, in lieu of any attempts at rekindling their once-cherished relationship. There were no parties or cakes. No fireworks or decorations. No cards or presents. No gatherings or songs.

After Uzuri's death, the Aseyori family did not receive any guests and there was no memorial service or funeral. The city government named the local football training grounds after Uzuri, and spent three days adding fertilizer and water to green up the field for a solemn ribbon-cutting ceremony. It was a beautiful program. The Aseyori family was not in attendance.

In the several days after Uzuri's murder, the Aseyori home was mostly dark. Ukweli did not eat for two days and only left his bedroom to use the bathroom. He broke his fast on the third day with a waffle, but he cried trying to eat it and ran upstairs to vomit. Mara did not leave her room for five days, not even to use the bathroom. Kobe put a diaper on her because she was not able to get out of bed. She may not have survived except for Kobe giving her bottled water and cans of nutritional shakes. He gave her sponge baths in the bed and sang Jill Scott songs while he brushed her hair. On the fifth day, Mara got up and took a shower. She brushed her teeth, got dressed, and headed downstairs. She got to the second step, sat down, and cried for an hour and ten minutes. Then she got up, and joined Kobe at the table in the nook.

"Would you like coffee, dear? I'm so happy to see you moving around. You're so beautiful."

"I can't believe she's gone, Kobe."

"I know. Me neither." He got up to get her a cup of coffee.

"Tell Ann that she wins."

"I'm sorry?"

"She wins. They win. The Company wins. They took my baby and they won't stop there."

"Those were rogue torqs, Mara. The Company had nothing to do with the invasion."

"Rogue?! She—You know what? Believe that if you want to, Kobe. It doesn't matter now anyway."

"What are you saying, Mara?"

"I'm saying that I'll cooperate. They don't have to question my commitment anymore."

"Mara . . . I don't think . . ."

"Just stop it! Stop it, Kobe! We know what that night was about, and we know what they were here to do. I told you that there would be resistance, and there will be, but it won't be from me."

Kobe placed the coffee on the table in front of her and returned to his seat. "How long do you think it will be before you are ready to move?"

"Kobe, just tell me what to do and where to be. I won't be an obstacle anymore."

"Mara, it doesn't have to be—"

"Where are they moving us?"

"Uhh, London. Islington."

"Give Ann the engine designs. I won't put Ukweli in danger any further."

"Kweli isn't in any . . ." he sighed. "We can leave whenever you're ready."

The Lagos Island estate held the darkest of memories for

the Aseyori family. Even amid so much pain, Mara couldn't bring herself to walk away from the house with Uzuri's room. The family would eventually move to London, but not until two years later. Ukweli completed his middle school work in Lagos online and only left the house to practice football and kendo with his trainers. He began having severe headaches. He no longer swam. He no longer ate waffles. He no longer called his parents Papa and Mama. The light in his soul was gone. It had been replaced with fear, anger, and darkness.

The Company exploded in popularity as torqs excelled in sports, politics, movies, real estate, and medicine. Torqs were rich and famous. The Company was playing the long game, and it was working. The Conference of Bishops broke away from the Vatican to join the world religion movement and, as a result, Bishop Xavier Dunnan, the chairman of the Conference, was named the first Grand Sovereign of the Movement. He would unite the world in the name of the most honored prophets, Jesus, Mohammad, Buddha, Gandhi, etc. His slogan was, "Love, Peace, and Sharing." The Company only had two rules concerning religion, "The Universe is the only deity, and no name shall be considered higher than any other." Honor all names. Worship no name. After all, the first step toward world peace was world equality.

The Company worked to keep the public informed to help calm fear and doubt. For instance, symbiotes could only inhabit a human machine with the willful cooperation of the human. Symbiotes could influence anyone, but humans could only take advantage of special abilities if they allowed inhabitation.

Symbiotes are divided into class and rank, just like most military or law enforcement sectors. Ghosts and ghouls are the bottom class. They mostly influence children and the elderly. Specters are the middle class and have the most special abilities. They can influence anyone, but are only allowed to inhabit adults. The highest class are the witches. They very rarely inhabit because they have the most unique ability of all, manifestation. They don't need to torq or influence to have an impact. This protected the highest class. If a human host died while inhabited, the symbiote would dissolve into a mist and cease to exist. Witches can participate in society as they are. They can take any form, usually the one that would receive the greatest public, human acceptance. Ann Jefferson was the highest-ranking witch and, as such, did most of the public appearances on behalf of the Company. As torqs had more success, more humans trusted the Company and made themselves available to be inhabited. One great world. One great love.

In April 2034, almost two and a half years after Uzuri's murder, the Aseyori family moved to England.

7

LONDON

The Aseyori family moved to the Camden Passage neighborhood in the London borough of Islington. The situation fit perfectly into the new, rigid family dynamic. Kobe and Mara continued their groundbreaking research at the Quantum Science and Technology Institute at University College London under the watchful eye of the Company. The spouses often spent ten or more hours in the same room without acknowledging the other's presence. They only spoke when their collaborative efforts required it. Their work at the university provided the resources they needed to maintain the growing space between them. They loved each other but were also disgusted with each other. They needed each other and they both knew it and they both hated it.

Ukweli enrolled at Highgate School in Haringey. Kobe and Mara were impressed with the academic reputation of the school and Ukweli submerged himself in the multitude of available activities. The school was twenty minutes by car or forty minutes by bus and tube (with a ten-minute walk from the station). Though the car was quicker and made sense during rainy days, Ukweli often chose to take the tube. Kiera took the tube.

Kiera Michaels was born in May 2020, in Atlanta. Her father grew up in Brazil, and he played football in the youth system before getting his break in the MLS. He became a star striker for Atlanta United before signing a big contract with Tottenham the same year Kiera was born. Kiera's mother was born and raised in New Delhi, a model, an actress, had a fitness fashion line, created an activewear cosmetics line that "doesn't run when you do," and was known for doing her own stunts in action movies. Kiera's dad said Tyler Perry was his personal friend and had introduced them. Her mom said they met at a charity function at Tyler Perry's house, but they didn't know him personally. Kiera embraced all aspects of her mixed culture. She loved yuca root and curry. She loved modeling and football and closely followed the Hotspurs, as did all students at Highgate. Like Ukweli, Kiera was good at a lot of things, loved to compete, and had acclaimed, accomplished parents. Unlike Ukweli, Kiera grew up in London and knew her way around.

Unlike Ukweli, Kiera had always been an only child.

Ukweli was in the park at Duncan Terrace watching the colorful boats in the canal when he saw Kiera for the first time. She was in the grass dribbling a football. He thought she looked like a sunset in Wakanda, the kind T'Challa took Killmonger to see right before he died.

"Hey!" Kiera jogged to the edge of the grass near the fence. Ukweli didn't notice that she spoke. "Hey, kid." She spoke softer since she was closer. Ukweli looked around to avoid embarrassment in case she wasn't talking to him. "Yes, you. Do you play?"

"Me?"

"Yes," she chuckled. "Do you play football?"

"Yeah."

"You think you can get it by me then, hmm?"

"I can." Ukweli shook his head as he answered.

"Ooo, quite confident, are you? Don't just sit there, then. Come have a go."

"Okay." Ukweli got up and walked to the gate in the corner. He didn't have his boots but he didn't figure he would need them to get the ball past a girl. He was right. He showed no mercy as he put the ball in the imaginary goal on the fence, time and time again. The more he scored, the more she demanded he do it again.

He only stopped because there was no fun in the lack of challenge she provided. He returned to his seat while Kiera yelled that he was a chicken for not giving her one more try. *Cute and crazy*, he thought as he returned to the park bench.

"Okay, so you're pretty skilled. Where do you play?" she asked, still inside the gate.

"I just moved with my parents from Nigeria. I played for the Super Eagles' development there."

"Does your dad play?"

"Haha, no way. My mom was a good player before she got hurt. They both work at the university."

"Do you live nearby?"

"Yeah, Clock Tower Mews."

"Oh, right. We live over on Barnsbury. Where do you go to school?"

"I start at Highgate in September."

"No way! That's my school! It's a great place. You'll love it. You'll certainly qualify for the football team there."

"Nah, my coach set me up to train with the Hotspurs, but I'll do kendo and squash at the school."

"Well, pardon me, Big Ben! My dad played for them. I

don't know anything about kendo or squash though." She paused. "We have a great big pool at Highgate. Do you swim?"

"No."

"You can't swim?"

"I didn't say I couldn't. I said I don't."

"You don't because you can't."

"I can."

"Then why don't you?"

"I don't like to."

"The only kids who don't like to swim are kids who can't swim."

"And me, I guess."

"Whatever. What's your name, kid-who-can-swim-but-doesn't?"

"Ukweli."

"Is that your only name, like Adele?"

"Ukweli Aseyori."

"I'm Kiera. Kiera Michaels. Nice to meet you Ukweli."

"Uhh, you too."

"Hey, give me one more try. If I can't stop you, I'll buy you a pastry at Kipferl."

"I don't eat sweets. Look, I gotta get home. I guess I'll see you around."

"Fine. Be a chicken then. Later."

Ukweli walked away from that first meeting in silence. He was so certain he would never meet anyone like Uzuri. The thought made him tear up and he walked faster, just in case Kiera was following.

SUMMER 2034

Ukweli did what he could to be wherever Kiera was, without letting Kiera know he wanted to be where she was.

He sat in the pizza shop at the corner of Barnsbury and Upper and waited for her to come outside so they could "accidentally" run into each other. He did this until it became less of a coincidence. They went to the movies and the mall together. They worked on football skills, together. They spent so much time together in the summer that it made Ukweli uncomfortable.

Ukweli liked that Kiera wanted to see him. Ukweli didn't like that Kiera *expected* to see him. He purposely broke his phone, got a new one with a new number, and did not share it with Kiera. He stopped going to the pizza shop on Barnsbury and Upper. He stopped going to the movies and the mall. He worked on his football skills alone.

The International Olympic Committee announced in June that Lagos would play host to the 2040 Olympic Games! Led by the Company, the oil discovery and production in Lagos tripled after the Reveal, and proceeds exploded. Thanks to the natural resources of the region, the technological advancements provided by the Company, and the torqs running the central government, Nigeria was able to win an underdog bidding system. The government of Nigeria pledged $15 billion in upgrades, which included a new stadium, new training grounds and facilities, and a new entertainment district in downtown. Ukweli made it chief among his goals to be on the roster for the Super Eagles as they simultaneously celebrated the Olympics and Nigeria's eightieth Independence Day.

FALL 2034

Ukweli enjoyed Highgate. The campus was old but nice, up-to-date in the important areas. The adults were very accommodating and treated Ukweli like many of the other students whose parents were considered high priority. He found many of his classmates to be spoiled and uninteresting, perhaps not unexpected at an elite school. Some annoyed him so much, he got a headache every time they were around. He tried extra hard to avoid those kids.

Though he had no intentions of making any new friends, he couldn't avoid everyone. Adam was in the squash club, and he was a good player. He wasn't as skilled as Ukweli, but he was just as competitive, and they made each other better. Paul was his jujutsu partner most days. He was competitive but kind of a practical joker. He was generally more interested in fun than winning, but he was also very skilled, so Ukweli overlooked his silliness. Ukweli considered taking entomology when he learned that Kiera was taking it, but he didn't like bugs and he particularly hated spiders, so he took an extra foreign language instead. He wasn't sure if he would actually ever need Spanish or Japanese, but he probably wouldn't need the Pythagorean theorem either.

Jackson Connaught was Highgate's most popular student. He was handsome and his family was very wealthy, heirs to a famous hotel chain associated with the royal family. He was born in New York, in the US, while his parents were there, considering proposals for new hotel properties, so he possessed dual citizenship—though he hadn't been to America since he was an infant. He was one of the best students on campus, the school's top chess player, and a kendo Nidan. He was the first person to best Ukweli in a competition.

The only thing larger than his trophy case was his ego. He was very spoiled, but he trained hard. He was ambitious and often talked about taking over the world, like a cartoon villain. Ukweli found him to be the perfect kendo sparring partner, except that Ukweli always got a headache before their training sessions. He couldn't explain it, it would sound like an excuse anyway, and he didn't understand it. He just learned to push through it.

Ukweli mostly kept to himself, as his friends and classmates mostly respected his space. He did, however, find it relieving to spend leisure time with Adam and Paul, playing video games or working out. He didn't talk to Kobe and Mara very much, even at dinner, so it was nice now and again to speak words to another human.

FALL 2035

Ukweli was finally starting to grow into his body. His confidence made sense. Maybe his grandfather was right. He genuinely enjoyed working hard at training. His swagger grew along with his body. Other students were now able to see in him what he always saw in himself. Kiera noticed too. They started to spend time together again, and Ukweli regretted allowing fear to push him away from her the first time. She was beautiful, smart, and confident. She was the best player on Highgate's football team and Ukweli considered her worthy of his time away from training. Ukweli cleaned his room whenever he knew Kiera was coming over to study and it dawned on him that he should just keep his room clean all the time so as not to allow Kiera the satisfaction of thinking she had the authority to dictate his standards. It was important to Ukweli that Kiera thought of him as a person of excellence. It was even more important that Kiera didn't think it had anything to do with her.

Ukweli enjoyed spending time with Kiera and he really didn't mind that she knew it. He just learned to give himself options to create space from time to time. Whenever he noticed himself feeling bottled up, he avoided the nuclear option and instead chose subtlety. He spent a little more time with Adam and Paul, training or playing video games or watching old kung fu movies. This allowed his relationship with Kiera to really flourish. Kiera was not his girlfriend. Her parents wouldn't allow it and Ukweli didn't want it. She was his best friend though. While he didn't allow himself to be vulnerable with her, he figured if he ever got to a place where he could cry about Uzuri, Kiera would probably be the only person he would tell.

Ukweli adjusted well to life in Islington. He trained at the Tottenham Hotspur Football Club Academy and even saw a little action with the U18 team. He trained in kendo. He trained in jujitsu. He enjoyed playing squash. He spent time with Kiera and Adam and Paul. He did not spend time with Kobe and Mara. He didn't deliberately avoid his parents, but their schedules rarely seemed to provide opportunities for quality family time and neither Ukweli nor his parents went out of their way to be accommodating.

Kobe and Mara went to work every day. It was important to Kobe that the Company was pleased with their work. It was important to Mara that the Company did not interfere with her son. Mara wanted Ukweli to enjoy a childhood free of the expectations of the Company. The Company was not pleased with Mara's desire for space.

SPRING 2036

Ukweli and Kiera's relationship was strained again. He was competing for Tottenham U18 and she was competing for Highgate football. Ukweli decided that he didn't have time to go to the spring formal, so Kiera went with Jackson Connaught. Ukweli didn't like it, but he couldn't be honest about not liking it. Frustrated, he once again went nuclear. New phone. New number. Kiera was really just a distraction anyway.

FALL 2036

If Ukweli had one complaint about Highgate, it was certainly the insistence that everyone participated in interest groups and scholastic clubs. There was a group at Highgate for almost every passion; sewing, writing, photography, cosmetology, backgammon, hot yoga—pretty much every activity had a club. They had a club for people who loved the outdoors for hunting and fishing and a different club for people who loved the outdoors for animal rights and *hated* hunting and fishing.

It was well-known that Oxford, Cambridge, and Harvard were all phasing out standardized testing as a measure of college readiness and were, instead, focusing more on extracurricular activities. The more clubs you were in showed you could manage your time and were ready to move on to the next level. Ukweli never understood why you needed to be a Squawker—that's what they called themselves—just to go into the woods to watch birds though. He joined the clubs for his sports, and Paul talked him into joining Highgate Crew. They had an intense rivalry with St. Paul's and the Henley Regatta proved to be a worthwhile endeavor. So, in addition to participating in clubs for football, kendo, squash, jujutsu, rowing, young politicians, and PlayStation FIFA (there was a separate club for Xbox FIFA), Ukweli also joined the bird-watching club. Kiera Michaels was a Squawker, and Jackson Connaught was a Squawker too.

SEPTEMBER 23, 2036

The Squawkers took a field trip to Kensington Gardens. Ukweli was quite sure he had never been in a setting like this one. He spotted ten different kinds of birds, wrote descriptions of their calls, and took pictures of the ones that would sit still long enough. He spent the remainder of his time carefully observing Jackson Connaught. It was easy to see that Jackson was interested in Keira. Most students were interested in Kiera. Ukweli watched Jackson. Jackson watched Kiera. Kiera watched Ukweli.

Ms. Medina, the Squawkers faculty sponsor, came over to Ukweli to check on his progress.

"Isn't this just a lovely park?"

"Yes, ma'am."

"Did you have places like this in Nigeria? I would imagine you didn't. We have the best parks in the world."

"Ahh, no, ma'am. Nothing like this."

"Have you been able to see any birds?"

"Yes, ma'am. I took pictures."

"Oh, good. I just love our beautiful parks. Parks are the combination of the two most wonderful things on earth, science and nature. Kiera, have you seen many birds?"

Ukweli had been unaware that Kiera was standing behind him.

"Yes, Ms. Medina. They're all over the park so they're pretty easy to see."

"Oh, that's good. I know it's so easy to get distracted by *all* of the sights here in the park. So many things can . . . pull our attention away from our assignment."

"Yes, ma'am. I'll see if I can find a few more."

As Ms. Medina walked toward the pond, Ukweli turned to face Kiera.

"She really likes the parks."

"I didn't take a jock like you for a bird watcher. A true Renaissance man, huh?"

"What is that?"

"Nothing. Send me three of your bird pictures."

"Cheater."

"Whatever. Give me your phone."

As Ukweli handed his phone over to Kiera, he felt a familiar pressure on his temples. He winced and reached for his forehead as the pain became sharper.

"You guys found all your birds?" Jackson asked, now standing beside Kiera.

"You okay?" Kiera looked at Ukweli with concern, ignoring the question. She handed his phone back to him.

"Yeah. I'll send these now." Ukweli walked away. He was certain Jackson was the cause of his headaches, but now he knew it had nothing to do with their kendo training. There was definitely something about Jackson that Ukweli didn't trust.

Kobe and Mara sat silently at the dinner table. Their condo in Islington was a nice space, very modern, but much smaller than their estate in Lagos Island. There was no pool. The dining room was formal, but there was only room for six at the table. The chef was excellent, owner of a local restaurant with a Michelin star, but even he struggled to extract drops of joy from the empty reservoir that was the Aseyori residence. When Ukweli arrived, Kobe and Mara had just been served the evening's first course of lobster thermidor.

"Hi, sorry I'm late."

"We've just been served, dear. You're just in time."

Ukweli walked toward the kitchen sink to wash his hands.

"How was your trip to Kensington? Are the gardens as beautiful as everyone says?" Kobe had not yet participated in the conversation.

"Yeah, it's really nice . . . if you like that kind of thing."

"And how was your training?"

"It was good. I beat Paul twice."

Ukweli sat down at the table and the attendant placed a cloth napkin on his lap and placed a small plate in front of him. The Aseyori family didn't have a butler or a full-time staff, but the chef traveled with a courtesy aide. He was considered max service. The family enjoyed their meal in silence until Kobe finally spoke.

"I need you home early for dinner Friday night. We're having guests."

"Yes, sir."

"Be sure you have a clean jacket to wear."

"Yes, sir."

Ukweli always had clean jackets because he only wore them at the request of his father. The school uniform did not require a jacket, only a collared shirt or a vest.

As the family continued to eat in silence, Ukweli thought back to the events of the day. He remembered his training victories over Paul. He thought of the gardens and the palace at Kensington and the birds. He thought of his headache and wondered what secrets Jackson was hiding. He smiled as he remembered the biggest win of the day. He, once again, had Kiera's number in his phone. He felt sure she would've given him her number had he asked. He didn't want to get it that way. He wanted Kiera to want him to have her number. Ukweli definitely liked Kiera, but Ukweli didn't like liking Kiera. He was confident this was the best way.

Ukweli gobbled his food and asked to be excused to study. He tried to stay calm as he walked around the corner to his bedroom. He sat in the chair at his desk, put on his headphones, and plugged his phone into the charger. He scrolled through his contacts, but he couldn't find "Kiera" or "Michaels." He looked through his entire contact list and came across an entry listed "The prettiest girl at Highgate." Okay, so she was clever. He decided that he needed to be funny and cool.

"Sorry for the delay. I've been trying to decide if I needed to assist a cheater." He texted.

Ukweli attached images of three of the birds that he found in the gardens. He leaned back in his chair and listened to Burna Boy while he waited for a response. It was only a few minutes later that his phone rang.

"Hello?"

"I was beginning to wonder if you were going to help me. Do you get pleasure from my agony?"

"No."

"Aww, that's so sweet."

"What?"

"You think I'm the prettiest girl at Highgate."

"It took me almost ten minutes to find you in my phone. You think you're funny."

"Of course I'm funny."

"I mean, you're not *really* funny like what . . . maybe not as funny as you think you could be."

"Okay, wow." She chuckled. "You're really bad at this. I guess no one can be good at everything."

"Huh?"

"Nothing. Listen, thank you for the pictures. I'll see you tomorrow."

SEPTEMBER 26, 2036

Friday, after school, Ukweli and Adam walked to the squash courts for monitored training. He explained to his coach that he would have to leave practice early because his parents expected him home to greet their dinner guests. That didn't stop him from thoroughly thrashing Adam first.

Ukweli was fast, strong, and aggressive. He felt a new energy and a fresh focus. He was in charge, as always, but he was starting to have fun again. He allowed himself to believe that things might not be as bad as they seem. He was at a good school. He excelled in his activities. He had managed to make friends, despite his best efforts to the contrary. Things were even getting better at home. His parents still didn't talk to each other very often, but they weren't arguing, and Mara hadn't seemed quite as stressed recently.

Ukweli didn't listen to music on the car ride home. He just looked out the window and tried to process the hope that was forming in his spirit. He wasn't even dreading dinner. Regardless of their strained relationship, he was very proud of his parents, and he knew that they loved him. He didn't generally enjoy dinners with their colleagues, but they knew they could trust him. He wouldn't let them down tonight.

Ukweli hopped out of the car, grabbed his bag, and thanked the driver. He walked up to the front door, and as he was going inside, he felt a sharp pain in his head. He shook it off as he lowered his bag to the floor by the stairs and walked into the living room. There he found his parents, seated together on the couch, and in the chair facing them was Ann Jefferson. Kobe and Mara seldomly spoke of the Company, and they spoke of Ann Jefferson even less.

"Ukweli, you remember Ann, right? She'll be joining us for dinner."

"Sure. Hi."

Ann turned toward Ukweli. "He just gets more and more handsome every day."

"Nice to see you again, ma'am."

"Ukweli, go ahead and wash up. Our guests should be here soon."

As he rounded the corner, Ukweli thought to himself,

more handsome every day, huh? How could she know that? He hadn't seen Ann since before they left Nigeria.

Ukweli showered and dressed and returned to the living room where his parents and Ann Jefferson remained seated. As he was about to sit, the doorbell rang and Kobe got up to answer the door. Mara looked at Ukweli and said, "Our guests tonight have been very friendly since we arrived in London. They are benefactors of the university and Ann said they have been very supportive of the Company. Oh yeah, they have a son who also attends Highgate. Maybe you know him."

Ukweli felt his eyes drop as the pain returned briefly, but intensely, to his head. He lifted his face just in time to hear Kobe say, "Ukweli, these are our friends Charles and Bailey Connaught and their son, Jackson."

Charles Connaught dominated the dinner conversation. He considered it an honor to have dinner with Kobe and Mara in their home and reiterated his and his family's commitment to the Company. He had always been confused by religion and wasn't confident in his ability to profitably manage his father's fortune, so the Company provided solutions and support for both concerns and the Connaught clan was thriving. The Connaught Hotel was voted the best hotel in London by Conde Nast and Travel and Leisure and there was talk of a second facility in New York. Bailey managed the boutique, spa, and restaurant in the hotel. It was Jackson, though, who had received the greatest benefit from the Connaught family's relationship with the Company. As the two families sat at the dinner table (they squeezed in an extra seat for Ann), Charles began to speak of Jackson's experience with inhabitation.

"Wait," Mara spoke up. "I thought the Company only inhabited adults. Jackson is in high school. He's a child!"

"Jackson has been able to do some truly extraordinary things," Charles said. "He is Highgate's most distinguished student. He is a kendo Sandan now . . . elevated beyond his age, undefeated in all levels of competition. He will soon achieve the title of chess Grandmaster. Jackson will lead the next generation into a period of unprecedented prosperity."

"Jackson will change the world." Ann joined the conversation in a way that made Mara uncomfortable. "Jackson has shown a commitment to the Movement that has elevated him to a higher level of being."

Ukweli felt the anger rising in his spirit. He wanted to leap over the table and choke Ann or Jackson or Charles or anybody. "You're a torq!"

Jackson stayed seated and calm while his father explained. "The two of you could be brothers. I only wish you could know the power and freedom he feels. Your parents were founding members of the Company, so you were meant for this Ukweli."

Ukweli stood and looked at his parents. Kobe was ashamed but sort of hopeful. Mara was shocked. They could sense Ukweli's rage building. He slung his chair around and started walking toward his room. Just before he closed the door behind him, he heard Ann say, "Just let him go."

That explained how Jackson was able to beat him in Kendo. He couldn't explain why he got the headaches, but he knew it was caused by torqs. That was the moment Ukweli Aseyori officially became an enemy of the Company.

Ann Jefferson and the Company considered Ukweli a threat to the progress of the Movement. They knew that Ukweli didn't seek the spotlight and never assumed he would be an outspoken opponent. Their concern was that Kobe or Mara—especially Mara—would become sympathetic to his disdain and waiver in their resolve to fulfill the stated mission of the Movement, to help improve God's good world. They knew that Ukweli's rebellious attitude could be weaponized by the Resistance, and they couldn't afford for their top minds to be corrupted. Kobe assured Ann that Ukweli had no contempt toward the Company and that they could manage his perspective, which they thought to be temporary.

Ukweli buried himself in his schoolwork and his training. He kept his mind and body occupied. He went from the classroom to the squash court, to the weight room, to the pitch in the city for work with the Hotspurs. The next day, he would train in jujutsu and kendo before heading to the canal to work in one of the boats.

He maintained his friendships with Adam and Paul, but they could see a darkness in him that wasn't present before. He was always competitive, but not like this. He treated practice days like tournaments. He often struggled to find jujitsu sparring partners because he had become increasingly brutal in his attacks. Ukweli trained at four a.m. before school, and very often didn't go to bed until after ten p.m., following a final late-night training session. He had no social media presence and cared nothing for social events. He felt responsible only for himself and the memory of his murdered sibling. He trusted no one. He carried an ever-growing reservoir of rage and hatred that served as efficient fuel for what he was becoming. That is the objective, after all . . . becoming.

DECEMBER 10, 2036

"Hello."

"Ukweli Aseyori, where have you been?"

"Kiera . . ."

"Don't 'Kiera' me. Why haven't you been answering your phone?"

"I've been training."

"Till ten?"

"Yes."

"I'm not just talking about tonight though. You haven't answered your phone for days."

"I've been training."

"What's up with you?"

"Nothing."

"Seriously, Mason said you broke someone's jaw sparring. He said the teacher kicked you out of practice."

"Yeah, so?"

"Adam and Paul said they haven't talked to you outside of training."

"I've been busy, Kiera."

"Oh, I'm so sorry for taking up your precious time."

"It's not like that. You don't understand."

"Then what is it like, Ukweli? What don't I understand? If you mean that I don't understand why you freak out and ghost me, you're right. I don't understand."

"You just don't get it." Call ended.

The next day, Kiera found Ukweli on the squash courts during lunch. She knew he saw her sit down but didn't acknowledge her presence there. She watched his movements which had become very aggressive. When his opponent questioned a call, Ukweli threatened to break his nose. The kid quickly grabbed his things and left the courts. Ukweli turned around and sat down on the bleachers near Kiera, grabbing a towel.

"How often do your foes leave crying?"

"Once is more often than they should."

"You weren't in class this morning."

"I've learned Japanese. That class doesn't help."

"Look, I don't know what's going on with you, but you're starting to alienate your friends. Are you not concerned about anyone else?"

"No."

"Really? No one else?"

"No."

"Wow. So I guess you don't have time for the Homecoming dance Friday either? Because you haven't said a word to me about it."

"I'm not going to the dance, Kiera."

"Yeah, I figured. That's why I said yes when Jackson asked me if I would go with him."

"You're going to the dance with Jackson?"

"Oh, that got your attention, huh?"

"Do what you want. I don't care."

"I know. You've made that clear. Look, I just don't like seeing you push people away who care about you."

"I'm good, Kiera."

"I don't deserve this. You owe me better."

"Enjoy the dance."

"Jerk."

Ukweli returned to the squash court and continued training alone.

One week later, Ann Jefferson announced that the Company would be offering opportunities for younger minds to be inhabited, a pivot from the original briefing.

Standing beside Ann was Jackson Connaught. Ann explained that Jackson was motivated but polite and empathetic. He excelled at his schoolwork and activities, but also maintained very productive relationships. Jackson spoke about his new confidence and his higher standards. He, along with his parents, announced the formation of a scholarship at Highgate and one at Oxford University, in Jackson's name, and the formation of a charity to provide healthcare for school-aged children in Islington who couldn't afford it.

MAY 2038

Jackson Connaught graduated from Highgate School as the valedictorian, a chess Grandmaster, and was voted "Most Likely to Succeed." His graduation address included the surprise announcement that he would be pursuing a civil engineering degree from the Georgia Institute of Technology in Atlanta. Kiera accepted a scholarship to join the women's soccer team at Georgia State University, conveniently located in close proximity to Georgia Tech.

Kiera never stopped caring for Ukweli, but she was uncomfortable with the growing shadow that surrounded him. She was even more concerned with the fact that he seemed to be embracing it.

Adam and Paul headed for the states too. Adam joined the squash team at Stanford while Paul became a member of the jujutsu club at Notre Dame and rowed for Fighting Irish Crew.

Ukweli lost touch with Kiera once she went to Atlanta, though he saw her once on television in the background at an announcement made by the Company concerning the population increase—which they accredited to the world peace provided by the unified world religion and the technological advancements that gave millions more citizens access to clean water and healthy food options. "The Universe has allowed the human race to thrive in its great peace," Ann said.

Ukweli managed to keep in touch with Adam and Paul, admittedly through no actions of his own, from across the Atlantic. After Highgate, Ukweli enrolled in Oxford and played professional football for Tottenham Hotspurs. He continued to train in kendo and jujutsu, though his time constraints forced him to leave squash and rowing behind.

Ukweli didn't have hobbies, only pursuits, and at the forefront was the acquisition of enough physical, financial, and political power to destroy the Company. Ukweli loved his parents, but their connection to the Company, and his hatred for it, planted a solid barrier between them. Ukweli left his parents' condo in Islington and moved into an apartment in Wood Green near the Hotspurs training grounds, which made it necessary to complete his work for his professors at Oxford remotely. Ukweli was ambitious and focused. He pursued his Oxford degree in politics and international relations.

8

TOTTENHAM

At age nineteen, Ukweli had his own luxury apartment in Wood Green and was a rising star midfielder for the Hotspurs. He developed a reputation in North London as a focused but eclectic recluse. Ukweli didn't mind this characterization since he did have to isolate more than his teammates because of his age and his academic requirements. During his rookie season with the first team, the Spurs tried, unsuccessfully, to limit his media availability. None of this, however, kept Ukweli from fully embracing his new social role as a mysterious millionaire playboy. At six-foot-four and two-hundred-ten pounds, Ukweli was a reluctant cover model for many of the most widely read local and international sports and entertainment magazines.

While Ukweli did not love the public space, nor the notoriety that came with being a professional footballer, he grew to appreciate the bevy of lasses that made themselves available to London's next big thing. He had no desire to etch out time for feelings, but he fully embraced the evolution of casual relationships. A Canadian magazine coined the term "decontracte au passage" to describe the current atmosphere of cultural sexual freedom.

Ukweli was cold when it came to his initial dealings with women. He really didn't see the benefit of maintaining social bonds when they didn't contribute to his ability to make ground on the Company in some way. While he didn't embrace the notion of romance, he welcomed the carnality of casual sex. He knew that his mother would strongly disapprove of his lifestyle in the city, but without the support of the Bible she made him study in his youth—thanks primarily to her and his father's relationship with the Company—he was free to explore everything the Universe had to offer.

As calculated and efficient as Ukweli was at sex, he was equally cold and robotic when it came to dealing with the post-coital emotions of the female species. Ukweli had a standing agreement with a local ride-hailing driver, who provided breakfast and a ride home for any unsuspecting young lady waking up disappointed and alone in the empty Wood Green apartment following an escapade with the latest cover model for *Ape to Gentleman* magazine.

NOVEMBER 10, 2039

One evening, after training, Ukweli decided on shrimp fried rice for dinner. He walked to the Chopstix on High Road, placed his order at the counter, and had a seat on the bench by the exit doors. After a couple of minutes, he was joined by a beautiful young lady. He could feel her attention on him. She cleared her throat.

"Excuse me. Are you the new striker for the Spurs?"

"I am new, and I play for the Spurs, but I'm not a striker."

"I'm sorry. I'm not too familiar with global football but I

thought I recognized your face from the advertisements. I'm Hope, by the way."

"No worries. Ukweli. Have you been to this restaurant before?"

"Yes, it's one of my favorites. They have the best fried dumplings."

"I'll try to remember that next time."

"Look, they have the best fortune cookies too. Here, this one's yours." She grabbed a cookie out of the cardboard box by the register.

"What do you mean, it's mine?"

"Fortunes belong to specific people at specific times. This one is yours."

"Hmm, okay. Thanks, I guess?" He put the fortune cookie in his pocket.

"No problem. Well, my food is ready. I'll see you around, Ukweli. Good luck this season."

"Thanks."

As the young lady turned and walked out of the door, the attendant handed Ukweli a white plastic bag and said, "Thank you for your business, Mr. Aseyori. I hope you will enjoy it."

"I'm sure I will. Can I get soy sauce?"

"Yes, sir. Soy and duck are in the bag, along with cutlery and chopsticks."

"Awesome. Thank you."

Ukweli took the bag and headed out the door. As he was walking, he became curious about the fortune cookie Hope had given him. He honestly thought she was flirting but she left abruptly, so he let the assumptions pass. He reached into his pocket and took out the cookie. He put his left hand through the holes at the top of the plastic bag so he could grab the cookie with both hands. He stopped on the sidewalk and tore open the clear, plastic packaging, and held the cookie. Nothing special. Just a regular fortune cookie. He broke the cookie open and grabbed the fortune. *A specific person at a specific time,* he thought to himself. He dropped the broken cookie into the trash and unrolled the fortune.

You are in grave danger. Trust no one. —Hope

Ukweli quickly lifted his head and searched his surroundings. He did not see Hope or anyone that looked suspicious. He squeezed the fortune paper in his hand and started walking toward his apartment. The short walk home seemed to last hours. When he finally arrived at his building, he moved cautiously to the elevator and hit the top button. He got off and grabbed his keys and walked toward his door, but was startled when his phone rang.

"Hello?" He was breathing rapidly.

"Hi, sweetie. It's Mama. Are you okay?"

"Yeah, I'm fine. Thanks."

"Oh, that's good. I worry about you these days, living in the city alone."

"I really am fine. Just busy."

"Oh, I know, sweetie. I'm not going to hold you. I just wanted to call and encourage you."

"Yeah?"

"I know that things can get tough when you're in the spotlight. I just want you to hold on to hope. Listen to hope when it speaks to you. I love you, dear. Enjoy your rice."

NOVEMBER 12, 2039

Jackson Connaught sat at a back table in the Waffle House on fifth street in downtown Atlanta. You could barely see through into the restaurant, thanks to the crude artwork using the windows as a translucent canvas. Aside from one painting of a yellow jacket mascot, the building was otherwise decorated to celebrate the Thanksgiving season. He was sipping a black coffee when Kiera walked in.

"Hey, sorry I'm late. My chem exam went over."

"I haven't been here long. We need to order though. I can't stay."

"Really? Again?"

"I know. I'm sorry. I'll make it up to you."

"That's the third time this week. They're putting too much on you."

"No. The Movement has so much momentum and they want to keep it going. Plus, the intel on the Resistance shows their numbers are growing too. People are choosing, Kiera. They're choosing now, so it's important that we reach as many people as we can."

A waitress approached the couple. "Y'all ready to order?"

"Yes," Kiera spoke up. "Let me get an egg white omelet with the fruit medley and a glass of water, please."

"What the hell, Kiera? You invite me to brunch at Waffle House and you order rabbit food?"

"C'mon, you know I have practice. I can't be running around all smothered and covered."

"Then why would you . . . anyway, I've trained hard all week, so I'll have a Philly omelet and a waffle please."

"You gon' stick with coffee?"

"Yes, thanks. And we'll need these to go." Jackson paid for the food and grabbed the bags. "C'mon, I'll drop you off." The pair got into Jackson's truck. The satellite radio was on and tuned to the world news station.

"Look, you wouldn't sit and eat with me. The least you can do is let me listen to some music on the way."

He obliged and changed the setting to 107.9 FM.

"You know, hip-hop doesn't keep you informed. Things are changing quickly, Kiera. You might want to try to keep up with what's going on."

"That's why I have you." She kissed him on the cheek,

increased the volume on the radio, and rummaged through the Waffle House bag to find her omelet. As he drove, she stuffed her face and sang along with the music. While Kiera was quite talented, even the most accomplished of singers sounds challenged with a mouth full of food.

"If you weren't so darn pretty, I swear. Don't get any of that on my seats, please."

She held her mouth open wide so he could see the half-chewed food. "Do you still think I'm pretty?"

They laughed.

He dropped her off at the training facility and headed to the hotel downtown.

When Jackson walked into the conference room at the hotel, he was greeted by Trevor Boseman, who had remained in the position of Chief of Staff in President Barney James' administration following the election in 2036. The Company insisted it would be beneficial to maintain continuity following the transfer of power. There were nine men seated at the large table engaging in separate discussions.

"Good afternoon, Jackson. Thank you for coming on such short notice."

"Well, it's not every day that the White House makes a request."

"Yeah, President James would've loved to have been here himself. He's very proud of you."

"Thank you, sir. I'm just trying to do my part to serve the Movement."

"You can take any seat. We're about to get started."

The lights dimmed and a projector at the front of the room flickered as it powered up. Boseman walked to the front of the room and began to greet the audience.

"Thank you all for being here. President James and Ann Jefferson send their regards. I know that everyone is pressed for time, so I'll be brief. We've kept a close eye on the Resistance and our intel has confirmed this. There is, in fact, an organized resistance hub, but it is no longer based in Italy. We're not sure what this means for the involvement of the Holy See. There seems to have been a fracture in the leadership, but we can't assume what that means. What we know is that they are planning to move their base here, to Atlanta. They're planning to challenge the authority of the Company by concealing their operations under the guise of an organization called the Church of the Seer."

"Do we know who is leading this 'church'?" one of the men asked from the middle of the table, as he made air quotes with his fingers.

"Remington Cross." There were troubled murmurs in the room.

"What?! Cross is still alive? What can we do about this?"

"Nothing . . . just yet. They are perfectly positioned to take advantage of our call for freedom and love. They're using our own charter against us. We don't think they even plan to operate as a church. They may just use the moniker to persuade the public that they're fighting for religious freedom. For now, Cross isn't to be touched. We'll just monitor the situation until we know exactly how they're planning to maneuver. Until something changes, we will continue to focus on recruiting and messaging. Jackson is entrenched here in Atlanta, and his recruiting efforts on the local campuses have been fruitful. We need to get his face in front of as many potential hosts as possible."

9

REMINGTON CROSS

Remington Cross was born Ren Tamaki in 1980 in Itoman on the southern point of Okinawa Island in Japan. His father was killed in a gang shootout in the city when Ren was an infant. His mom was a barmaid who attracted the attention of an American airman stationed on the island which eventually had Ren and his mom move to Chicago with her new husband when he was five years old. The airman adopted Ren, taking his last name, Cross. It is unknown if Ren got the name "Remington" from his love of guns or from the popular '80s tv show, but it stuck. Everyone called him Remington, except his mom.

He did not answer to Remi.

Cross had a tough time in school. He was smart—brilliant in fact—perfectly capable in the classroom. The problem, however, was that he loved to curse and fight. He didn't even have to be offended to let a few obscenities fly during a lecture or to haul off and punch a classmate in the face. He was rude and crude and his teachers and classmates alike hated to see him coming.

Things changed for Cross when, in the eighth grade, he was introduced to the US Army Reserve Officers' Training Corps. Every decision he made for the next twenty years would be to uphold and defend the Constitution. Cross was a part of Delta operations in the Middle East, Asia, and eastern Africa, and his distinguished military career took him on joint missions to six of the seven continents.

Cross retired from the military in 2019, however, following a congressional review of his methods after multiple accusations of unnecessary and inhumane brutality. Cross resolved to live the remainder of his life ridding the world of bullies, gangsters, warlords, and any person or organization who didn't share his worldview. He was considered a threat to every world government. He lived off the grid, conducting operations in South America, Europe, and Africa until 2030, when it was rumored he was killed during a cartel sting in Columbia. That was until he showed up alive and well as the first-ever Supreme Eye of the Church of the Seer in Atlanta.

His introductory press release video outlined the three core tenants of the Church of the Seer:

1. Rid the world of every rogue torq.

2. Expose the corruption and evil of the Dark Reveal.

3. Pursue a path of personal peace through service to the world.

The Church of the Seer would seek to apply pressure on the Company and all those who were on board with their missions. This meant possible trouble for President James and other world leaders. Remington Cross was a threat to Ann Jefferson and Jackson Connaught. He was a threat to Drs. Kabeyesi and Unimara Aseyori. He became an idol for Ukweli.

NOVEMBER 14, 2039

After his run-in with Hope and her fortune cookie, and the bizarre phone call with his mother, Ukweli decided on a morning stroll to the park. He needed to unclutter his mind from the events of the previous days. Additionally, he needed to offer time and space for the girl in his apartment to shower and leave. Honestly, he didn't even know who she was. She had just been waiting for him at his front door when he got home last night. As he walked, he contemplated the implications behind the warning Hope issued in the form of a fortune cookie. It wasn't lost on him that if Hope's warning was legitimate and he actually was in some sort of danger, for whatever reason, perhaps he shouldn't allow random women to spend the night with him. *I'm probably overthinking things*, he thought. He sat down on a bench in Wood Green Commons and watched people walk by, wishing Uzuri were there to help judge them, until a man he didn't know approached him a few minutes later.

"Ukweli Aseyori?"

"Yeah."

"You know why I'm here?"

"An autograph?"

"Actually, I'm more of an Arsenal fan."

"Then, no."

"My friends and I have been told that you got a problem with the Company."

"If you want to talk endorsements, you'll have to contact my agent."

"I got a message for you. If you want to keep playing football, keep your nose out of places it don't belong."

"Is this about the girl from last night? Dang. Is she your wife or something? Look, she was waiting for me at my front door. She didn't even tell me her name so . . ."

"No one cares about your strumpets. If you know what's good for you, you'll stay away from Hope."

"I don't know any Hope but—"

"If she contacts you again, just know that we're watching."

"Eww, bro. That's a little off my freak meter, but I guess whatever floats your boat."

"Yeah, just remember what I said. And go Gunners."

As the man turned and walked away, three other men came out from hiding and walked away with him. Kobe insisted that the torqs who killed Uzuri had gone rogue, but Ukweli saw them all the same. He didn't trust any of them.

Hope was right. Don't trust anyone. The problem was, he didn't trust her either.

SPRING 2040

Ukweli continued to grow in popularity as he performed with excellence on the pitch. The Hotspurs fell just short of the Premier League title, but they qualified for the Champions League, thanks to Ukweli's stellar play. He always knew he was being watched by the Company, but it became indistinguishable from the attention of the fanatics and fringe media. He learned to accept his current lot and knew that to really strike a blow to the Company, he would need to be much stronger financially and politically.

He didn't have the international alignments he knew he would need to be able to make a strong stand. He focused on finishing his degree and his continued training in jujitsu and kendo. He also worked on adding Italian to his list of fluent languages.

And there were women. Lots of women. Ukweli didn't subscribe to the abundance of psychological explanations for his attitude toward women and sex. He didn't like media attention, but he liked the attention that came from the media.

Ukweli knew that he missed his sister. He knew that, even though he didn't trust his parents, he missed them too. His age and, quite frankly, his quick rise to stardom on the pitch, made it difficult to bond with his football mates. He would have to find fulfillment in other ways until the right opportunity to avenge Uzuri presented itself. As fate or Unity would have it, that opportunity would come sooner than he expected.

JUNE 2040

Ukweli arrived in Nigeria for the first time since leaving for London to a hero's welcome. The festive atmosphere surrounding the arrival of the Olympic Games created emotional nostalgia in Ukweli. He felt a great deal of pride in his homeland and his hometown and was elated to join the Super Eagles roster for the games.

He had developed a cult following back home and participation in the Uzuri Aseyori Girl's Developmental Football League had skyrocketed. There was, however, a mixed reaction among his homegrown teammates. Some only wanted to win and were happy to see him. Some were jealous of his success and felt it was unfair he was given a provisionary position even though he hadn't worked with the team since his youth. They complained that he was really a British citizen and started calling him "UK." It was meant as an insult, but it stuck after some inquiring members of the media heard it. UK and his Nigerian mates performed admirably and made it out of the group stage only to lose to

Germany in the quarterfinals. The Nigerian government was grateful to Ukweli for the positive publicity and asked him to commit to participating in the 2042 World Cup, which he did.

Following the loss, Ukweli returned to London in time to see the horrific news that a bomb had been detonated in the central stadium at the closing ceremony in Lagos. Six people were killed and hundreds were injured. The Nigerian government took to the media to quickly condemn the act of terroristic violence, which they blamed on Remington Cross and the Church of the Seer. Cross quickly released a statement condemning the violence as well as the accusation, claiming that it is against the tenants of the Church of The Seer to employ state violence. No one was ever charged.

JULY 2040

Remington Cross sat in a chair behind a desk on the forty-fourth floor of One Atlantic Center. He slowly spun around to take in the view of the city at night, contemplating the consequences of his most recent decisions. He didn't care what happened to him. He feared no man. He didn't fear death. He had stared death in the face many times and emerged victorious. No doubt death would come to collect its tax eventually, so every day above ground was like icing on the cake. Only the mission mattered now.

He was so angry at the direction in which the world was headed, and he was discontented and embarrassed that the United States was leading the way, leading the world down a path of voluntary servitude and disguising it as freedom and love. He and his team had toppled government establishments for far less and he certainly had no plans to sit idly on the sidelines while his beloved America swirled into the toilet. His views concerning America had always been conservative, he saw imperialism as America's gift to the world. Though he had no care for religion, he was no one's liberal and would look for a fight to defend any individual's right to choose their own religion or to choose none at all.

At some point, he decided it was ridiculous to even use the words "conservative" and "liberal." *All people*, he thought, *fight for the freedoms that matter to them.* Some citizens want the freedom to have as many of whatever kind of gun they choose. Some want the freedom to choose their own reproductive rights. He personally did not believe in the immorality of abortion because he considered morality to be subjective. Some want the freedom to wear a mask. Some want the freedom not to wear a mask. Everyone finds peace in their own way, but they must be provided the freedom to discover that way for themselves. He was willing to die on that hill and he was willing to kill anyone who disagreed.

The Company had compiled a great deal of worldwide power in a very short time. This was unlike any enemy Cross had encountered before so he knew his moves would have to include a nod to subtlety, though that was not his calling card. Remington Cross was known in inner circles all over the world for being the most efficient, effective, and brutal commander since Genghis Khan. His teams were the best in the world and moved like ghosts. He never gave face-to-face orders. This protected the identities of his units and the integrity of the missions. In fact, there was only one person world leaders could identify as a known associate of Remington Cross.

Kelley Jack was born in Chicago fifteen years after Remington Cross and his family arrived in the states. She never knew her father, and her mother left her in a dumpster the same night she gave birth to her. Remarkably, she survived in the dumpster for two days, until she was spotted by a sanitation worker, who dropped her off at a local monastery.

Kelley was only five years old when she killed a man who was trying to rape her. Reports stated that she stabbed the man almost one hundred times, set his body on fire, and calmly walked away. She was eventually forced to leave the monastery. She lived on the unforgiving streets of Chicago for one year before joining a local gang. Despite her young age, she was sexed into the gang and became a contributing member, able to earn trust because of her innocent appearance. Two years later, authorities found seven members of the gang dead from stab wounds and no sign of Kelley Jack.

She reemerged three years later when Remington Cross caught her trying to break into his car. Kelley had it in her mind to kill Cross, but she found that his skill and brutality were even greater than hers. She woke up the following morning, bloody and sore in the back seat of his car. Cross admired her skill and tenacity, so he took her to live with him at the army base.

He raised her as his daughter, so she became a military brat. They were inseparable. By the time she was old enough to join the military herself, Cross had retired from the army and formed his own undercover unit, with Kelley being the chief strategic officer and the only member of the unit allowed to see Cross in person. Kelley had dark brown skin, long jet-black hair, and light brown eyes. Her beauty was surpassed only by her cunning and ruthlessness. It was Kelley, in fact, who gave Remington Cross the idea to establish the Church of the Seer as the focal point of the Resistance.

"You know, we'll need help with this, Kelley."

"You've never had a problem assembling a team before."

"No, that's not what I mean. We need a face. We need someone the whole world can get behind. We need someone the world will trust."

⑩

ALEXANDER SCOTT

FEBRUARY 14, 2041

Almost ten years after the Dark Reveal, Pope Gregory initiated the process of papal renunciation. The stress of the defense of the archives and the constant media attacks had taken its toll. Pope Incursus I became the first Greek to occupy the Holy See since Julius II in the early part of the sixteenth century. Incursus was energetic and ambitious, and the Company saw this as an opportunity to finally sway the Vatican to join the Movement.

Everyone was excited when Incursus announced that his first international trip would be to the United States. Things changed, however, when he was scheduled to arrive in Atlanta, not Washington, DC, and it was rumored that Pope Incursus was intending to make a progressive speech outlining a very aggressive campaign against the Company and against the Movement.

The fact that he was giving his speech at the Cathedral of Christ the King made it clear to the Company that it would not be a message supporting the worldwide unity they had achieved. Pope Incursus traveled to Atlanta with his security team and his camerlengo, Alexander Scott.

"I still feel we need to review the speech, your holiness. A lot is riding on public perception and your delivery may influence some fence-straddling minds."

"Settle yourself, Alexander. My message is God's message, and it will be received in the most appropriate way."

"Can I at least see it?"

"No, you cannot. Besides, it is not here with me. I have only written one copy and it remains in the bowels of the archives. I purposely did not produce any digital copies for fear of dissemination. You'll just have to trust my mind."

The motorcade made its way up Peachtree, toward "Jesus Junction," and came to a stop on the side of the facility. There were barricades in place to be sure that no one was able to get close to Incursus, but though they were a great distance away, the gathered crowds were quite large. The security detail moved quickly and positioned themselves to slip Pope Incursus into the rear entrance.

"Listen, Alexander, please don't trouble yourself. While we may have enemies, we are doing God's work. The world is changing, and we have a responsibility to stand firm despite the risks."

"Yes, your holiness."

A member of the security detail opened the door to give Pope Incursus just enough space to get out of the vehicle with Alexander Scott exiting behind him out of the same door. Pope Incursus placed both of his feet on the ground and stood, fighting the urge to wave a greeting to the crowd. Alexander slid to the edge of the seat and placed his right foot outside the door when he heard it. It sounded like a tire puncture.

Very suddenly, the scene, which was already hectic, turned fully chaotic as Pope Incursus collapsed to the ground. Alexander, shocked, sat frozen with one foot out of the car door. One of the security staff members shoved his head back into the car as two of the others grabbed the injured frame of Incursus and hastily flung him into the back seat on top of Alexander. Sirens blared as the motorcade raced off, narrowly avoiding fleeing pedestrians.

Alexander managed to sit up as he heard the staff screaming into the communication devices, "He's hit! He's been hit!" Alexander, now sitting up in the back seat with the pope's head on his lap, noticed for the first time that there was a small, bloody hole near the abdomen on the pope's white robe. He reached to touch it but was startled when Incursus grabbed his face.

"Al-ex-ander . . ."

"Yes, your holiness?" He tried not to sound panicked.

"Prepei na mou . . . yposchetheis."

"Sir?"

"The seer . . . the . . . seer . . . *einai o monos tropos."*

"Your holiness!"

Alexander watched in horror, through a cascade of tears, as Pope Incursus died there, in his arms, in the back seat of the car. He continued to hold his hand until they reached the ER at Piedmont. The team quickly extracted the pope and rushed him inside, but Alexander knew that he heard the last words he would ever hear from his friend and mentor. *The seer?* he thought to himself. He shook his head with the weight of the world on his chest and cried into his hands.

For immediate release:

From the desk of Ann Jefferson, Friend of the Movement

We are truly saddened by the tragic death of Pope Incursus I and our thoughts are with the friends, family, and loyalists who have chosen to remain tethered to their message. While we are confident that Pope Incursus was moving toward a prosperous future in collaboration with the Company, we are equally as convinced that those who seek to divide us will not be successful. Justice will be served. All accounts will be settled. Peace will be restored.

For immediate release:

From the desk of Remington Cross, Supreme Eye, Church of the Seer

The tragic assassination of Pope Incursus I is just the next step in a long line of control tactics by the Dark Reveal. There are those among us who intend to enslave us, and we at the Church of the Seer will not stand by and simply accept what we are given. This show of aggression toward one of our planet's most beloved religious leaders will not go unpunished. We are the Resistance. We are the Vision. We are the Response.

11

THE CHURCH OF THE SEER

A lexander Scott sat in a chair in the executive office at the Church of the Seer. Remington Cross stood behind the desk, looking out the window at the cloud cover that hovered over the waking city. Kelley Jack sat on the corner of the desk, seeming somewhat annoyed, staring at Alexander. The more she stared, the more fidgety he became. He couldn't look away though. He had a hard time matching her reputation to her face. Supermodel psychopath.

Remington turned to face Alexander but didn't sit.

"Are you sure that's what he said? The Seer?"

"Yes."

"And nothing else?"

"Ahh, yes, he said that it was our only way."

"The Seer."

"Yes, umm . . . yes, sir."

"I don't trust him." Kelley blurted in. "What if he's here just trying to feel us out?"

"Listen, I don't know why Incursus would send me to you. I'm just telling you what he said and I hope you'll know where to go from here."

"Your friends in Italy . . . what does the Vatican Counsel think of this?"

"I don't know. I have only told you the words. None of them know I'm here."

"Let's keep it that way for now. Return to Italy and go about your business as usual. I'll be in touch."

Alexander got up from the chair and walked quickly out of the office and down the hall to the elevator.

Remington spun his chair around and took a seat. Kelley stood and walked around to the back of the desk.

"You're just going to let him leave?"

"Yes."

"You know if they make him Pope, he won't be as accommodating as he is right now."

"Maybe. Or perhaps we'll have an ally. Either way, it's too early to press him. Remember that our war is not against the Vatican."

"Not yet."

"Run the recruitment clips. We're officially in phase three."

MAY 16, 2041

Ukweli sat in a coffee shop in Wood Green. Though he didn't drink coffee, he enjoyed the active atmosphere. People used coffee to get going and he liked being around ambitious people. He didn't talk to any of them though. He sat with his noise-canceling headphones covering his ears, even though there was nothing coming through them. His laptop browser had several open pages, including one with pan-seared duck recipes, one with the internet's humorous animated response to the search "elegant duck," and one open on the Georgia State University Women's Soccer homepage.

Ukweli scrolled through stats and photos from the Panthers' fall season. He wasn't surprised to see Kiera in a lot of the images. He received a text notification from his driver partner on his watch saying, "The nest is clear." He almost regretted ejecting last night's haul, but when you live a catch-and-release lifestyle, trophies represent evidence. At all times and in all situations, no matter how pretty or cool she might seem, prize fish must be returned to the lake.

Right at that time, a red light flashed in the corner of his computer screen and a new page automatically opened in a new window. This happened to all the open laptops in the café. A man appeared on the screen.

It was Remington Cross.

"Good morning, citizens. I apologize for the disruption. I'll be brief. My name is Remington Cross and I am the Supreme Eye of the newly established Church of the Seer in Atlanta. Some of you may have seen my materials before. I am sending this message out in the morning hours of every major city in the world as a personal invitation. I want you to join our movement! We have been waiting for the appropriate moment to give our message to the world, but the assassination of Pope Incursus I has shown us that we can't stand to wait any longer. If you're ready to make a difference and take our world back, click the red button in the upper right corner of your screen. You have ten seconds to decide. Don't pass up on the greatest adventure and responsibility of your life!"

Ukweli felt his heart rate quickly rising and it made him uncomfortable. What did this mean? He couldn't leave his career to join the Church of the Seer! He was living the dream of every man, in every part of the world. Why would he even consider giving all of that up? And for what? He knew nothing about Remington Cross. What was he thinking?

He clicked the red button. His screens closed. His computer powered down.

He closed his laptop and walked back to his apartment. He paced around a little, not sure what to do next. Surely this was not a big deal. All he did was click the button. He didn't sign any papers or anything. No problem.

He sat down and turned on the television. His phone rang. He turned the television off. The phone screen showed that the call was from Atlanta. Ukweli answered the phone.

"Hello?"

"Is this Ukweli Aseyori?" A female voice.

"It is."

"Hold on."

"Ukweli, hello. This is Remington Cross. How are you?"

"Fine."

"Before we begin, do you mind if I ask how your parents are?"

"I guess they're okay. We don't speak very often."

"They're still in London?"

"Yes, at the university."

"Good . . . swell. I'm a big fan of their work. Certainly, their genius exists outside of the influence of the Reveal. Nevertheless . . . I want to meet you. I think we can be a great help to each other."

"I'm not sure. I have a lot going on. I don't even know who you are."

"Of course, you're very busy, what with football and university and all. I won't take up much of your time and I promise I'll make it worth your while."

"What do you want me to do?"

"I would like to meet with you. I'll explain everything then."

"When?"

"There is a car outside. It will take you to my plane. I'll see you tonight."

Ukweli pulled back the curtain and saw a black SUV parked on the curb with a man in a gray suit standing beside the rear passenger door. He felt like he was beginning his life's greatest adventure, or maybe entering his final tragic moments. Perhaps the two were not mutually exclusive.

Ukweli quickly prepared a small duffel and headed to the car. The driver never spoke. He took Ukweli's bag and opened the door. Ukweli slid in and the driver closed the door behind him, gently placed his bag in the front seat, hurried to the driver's door, and got behind the wheel.

The ride to the airstrip was quick and quiet. They arrived at the plane and were greeted by three women dressed in black skirts and V neck blouses, with grey chiffon scarfs, and a pilot dressed in a gray suit like the driver. The plane was unassuming and elegant. They began to taxi and were off the ground less than five minutes after boarding. Once they were at cruising altitude, one of the women sat across from Ukweli.

"Hi, I'm Lacy. The other two attendants are Ginger and Crystal. Our flight is scheduled for eight hours and six minutes. We were informed you don't drink alcohol, so the Eye has arranged for you to enjoy imported Parisian spring water. Let us know if we have been misguided concerning this and we can get you whatever you like. Also, we have arranged a full-service massage during the flight. Simply let us know when you would like for that to begin. We also—"

"Now."

Ukweli walked into the executive offices of the Church of the Seer. His legs were still a bit shaky from the long flight. The office was bigger than Ukweli expected. He almost expected to speak to a screen instead of a real person, based on what he learned of Cross that day. There had been a man in a gray suit, like the driver and the pilot, waiting for him in the lobby of the building and he guided Ukweli to the elevator and down the hall.

Once they reached the door to the offices, he turned and walked back to the elevator. Ukweli walked in alone and was met by Kelley Jack. The two walked together through another short hallway and into another large room with a single desk. Standing next to it was the commanding figure of Remington Cross.

"Welcome, Ukweli. Thank you so much for coming at such short notice."

"It didn't seem I had much of a choice."

"I'm sure you understand, these matters are time-sensitive. We are very appreciative of your cooperation. I trust the flight crew saw to your needs?"

"Yes, they did. Quite impressive, your crew."

"Excellent. Can we get you anything now?"

"No, thank you. I would just like to know why I'm here."

"You're here because you clicked the red button."

"I don't understand."

"You watched the video and you clicked the red button."

"I'm the only person who clicked it?"

"Of course not. Millions of people clicked the button."

"Then I truly don't understand why I'm here."

"While millions of people in London, Paris, Madrid, Casablanca, and Lagos clicked the red button, only one person clicked the red button whose Nobel laureate parents opened the door to the Dark Reveal."

"So, I'm here so you can get to my parents?"

"Not exactly. You're here because we think you can help us. In fact, I think we can help each other."

"How so?"

"You want to punish the people responsible for your sister's murder and for destroying your family. I want to punish the people responsible for destroying my country and taking our freedom. As it turns out, those are the same people."

"My father said that Uzuri was killed by rogues."

"That is what your father was made to believe when, in fact, your sister was killed by a tactical team."

"Why would the Company want my sister dead? She was only nine."

"They weren't there for your sister. They were there to kill your mother."

Ukweli sat in silence, shocked by the revelation. Kelley began to speak.

"Your mom made a world-changing discovery, some type of engine. We don't know all of the details, but we do know that it was powered by a self-sustaining source, meaning technically, it could run forever."

"Why would the Company want to kill her for that? Couldn't they just take it?"

"They didn't want to kill her to take the engine," Cross said. "They wanted to kill her because she did it without them. Her mind was free."

"And a free mind is a dangerous mind." Kelley watched Ukweli closely as she spoke.

"Is that why they killed the pope? Because he had a free mind?"

"That's exactly why they killed the pope! That's why we have organized an offensive against them."

"We? The two of you are going to take down the Company?"

"I don't appreciate your tone." Kelley never looked away from Ukweli.

"Kelley . . . you'll have to excuse her. She is not very trusting."

Ukweli looked up at Kelley. He hadn't noticed the fury on her face. Her beauty hid it well. He decided that he should back off.

"What exactly do you need me to do?"

"Ukweli, we have operatives in training all over the world. We have simply been waiting for the right time to launch. We have been waiting for the right leader. We've been waiting for you."

"Me? I'm a footballer. I know nothing of military operations."

"You are a warrior and your entire life has been nothing but training for this moment in history. You will continue to train in combat, and Kelley will assist you in operations."

"But what of my life? My career? I still have a year at Oxford."

"You will return to London and compete with your mates in Tottenham. You'll finish at Oxford next spring. After that, you'll come and join us here, in Atlanta. We will continue your training and you will enroll in the public policy program at Mercer."

"Public policy? Mercer? Why more school?"

"Not only will you be a field general, but as the public face of the Church of the Seer, you will hold a political position as well. It is important that you understand the lingo of world politics. When you're prepared, you'll be perfectly positioned to strike a blow to the frozen heart of the Dark Reveal and, eventually, take my place here, as the Supreme Eye."

"So, what am I supposed to do now?"

"Focus on your season and your classes. Take advantage of your media opportunities. You must stay clean, though, above reproach—so no more random women. We can provide for your needs. After the Champions League in the summer, you will retire from English football and return to Atlanta to continue your training."

"How can I trust you? You obviously don't trust me."

"We do. We're counting on you."

"Kelley doesn't trust me."

"She does."

"How do you know?"

"You're alive."

OCTOBER 2041

Jackson Connaught pulled up to the Stonecrest Library and walked inside. Kiera was waiting inside and greeted him with a friendly hug. Things between the two had become strained lately. Kiera was finishing her final season on the soccer team and was preparing to graduate in December. Jackson was so busy with school and recruiting for the Company, he barely had time for anything else. He graduated from Georgia Tech two semesters early and had already begun graduate work.

The tiny bits of free time in their schedules rarely seemed to be in step, so they took opportunities, like this one, to spend time helping each other with their respective assignments, whether for school or the job. Jackson didn't know much about Remington Cross and the Company couldn't verify much of what they even thought they knew. He was too strong mentally to influence, he had his own agenda and life taught him the only voice he should obey was his own. He trusted himself completely. He trusted Kelley Jack conditionally. He trusted no one else.

Jackson was at the library to research Army Delta unit operations to see if he could get an insight into Cross's training.

"Thanks for meeting me here. I'm sorry about the bus."

"Nah, Jen dropped me off. It's cool."

"Oh, okay. You wanna grab a coffee or something before we get started?"

"No, I'm okay. What are we looking for again?"

"I need you to find everything you can on Army Delta missions in the twenty-tens. You won't find many specifics because everything they do is classified, but there may be an article about operations. The information may be dull, but every bit helps. Let me know if you can find anything at all."

"Wow, this guy really was off the grid, huh?"

"Yeah, big time. I just need to find something—anything that can give us an edge."

"Hey, can I ask you a question?"

"What's up?"

"Did you guys kill the pope?"

"What?"

"I'm saying—well, not me, but people are saying the Company killed the pope."

"Of course not. We had nothing to do with that."

"Well, people were saying that his speech would hurt the Company."

"No one knows what his speech would've done. He was newly appointed. He just as easily could've given us his full support. Now we'll never know."

"Hey, I'm just worried about you."

"I know. There's no reason to worry though. We're doing good work. We have nothing to hide. So please, dive into that microfiche and find something I can use."

FALL 2041

Ukweli returned to Wood Green living under a new set of rules. He now had a blossoming social media presence, thanks to the team put in place by Remington Cross. He wanted to be sure that Ukweli received maximum exposure for any and every accomplishment on and off the pitch. Ukweli attended more charity events. He was given contact information for five different women and he could call any or all of them at any time for any needs from cooking and cleaning to more amorous activities when he so desired. This meant no more random women, which seemed, for a while, to make the young women in the area desire Ukweli even more. He trained in football, kendo, and jujitsu with all of the passion and enthusiasm he had. He competed like a person who knew his career would soon end. He left it all on the field. He even got teary-eyed as he stood over a penalty kick and was taken back to the dream he had the night Uzuri was killed. He didn't understand why he got to live his dream while Uzuri's life was cut short. Sometimes, he felt guilty for enjoying things the way they turned out. He was leaving it all behind now. The English Premier season and the Champions League with Tottenham Hotspur, the 2042 World Cup with the Nigeria Super Eagles, and then the end.

JUNE 21, 2042

Jackson Connaught stood in the backyard of his home in the Oakhurst neighborhood in Decatur, just outside Atlanta's city limits. He preferred the contemporary style of the homes in College Heights, but the traditional homes in his community seemed like something his mother might feel comfortable visiting. She died just a few weeks after closing, so she never got to visit from London, but he didn't regret the purchase. It was growing on him. Having Kiera there with him helped a lot.

He lifted the lid on the grill to check the progress. Asparagus and sliced new potatoes. Tomahawk for him. Cedar plank salmon for Kiera. It was the perfect early summer meal for the big plans he had for that night. They would celebrate her great collegiate soccer career, toast to her graduation, and then she would certainly cry as he got onto one knee and presented her with the flawless, two-karat diamond ring in his pocket. That was the plan. It was a good plan.

The two of them sat at the table on the covered portion of the back porch. Jackson lit a candle and played soft music on his phone.

"I thought this was supposed to be a celebration." Kiera laughed.

"I'm just trying to set the mood," Jackson responded.

"What mood? Depressed? Play that new Brielle song. Let's turn this party up!" Jackson didn't care for pop music, but this was Kiera's special night.

"How's your food?"

"Oh, it's amazing! I swear you're a grill master. Kung Fu Joe should be paying you for using their grill."

"Maybe someday Ka-ma-do Joe will." They both laughed. "Kiera, I have something that I want to ask you."

"Okay?"

"You love me, right?"

"Jackson, what's this about?"

"Well, I was wondering—"

"Hang on . . . can you turn the tv up?"

"Huh?"

"It's the Champions League final. Ukweli is playing in it with Tottenham. I bet they'll win it this time."

"Oh, yeah, right . . . they probably will."

"Okay, what were you saying? Do I love you and blah blah blah?"

"Uhh, yeah, I just like to hear it sometimes."

"I love you, I love you, I love you! And I'll love you even more if you grab me another water."

"Of course."

"Thanks, babe."

Jackson got Kiera another water and watched Ukweli Aseyori and his hometown favorite Hotspurs win the Champions League title. He decided tonight was not the right night. He kept the ring in his pocket.

Two days later, Jackson watched, along with the world, as Remington Cross announced two new additions to his staff. Alexander Scott, former camerlengo to Pope Incursus I, was now Premier of Religious Freedom at the Church of the Seer. For the first time in public, Alexander Scott told the story of the final moments in the life of Incursus, and how he said, "the Seer" was the only way. Furthermore, the Church of the Seer would get the unconditional support of the Vatican in its fight against the Dark Reveal.

Cross then announced that his new CEO-in-waiting was Tottenham superstar, Ukweli Aseyori.

Ukweli, at the peak of his athletic prime and just two days removed from hoisting the Champions League trophy, announced that he was retiring from professional football at the conclusion of the World Cup to focus on his new passion; a return to justice. He informed the world that the people who murdered his sister were the same people who assassinated the pope. He also unveiled the new slogan of the Church of the Seer: "Peace Through Accountability."

Dr. Kabeyesi Aseyori received a text message. "Do we have your permission to consider him a threat *now*?"

(12)

ATLANTA

AUGUST 4, 2042

U kweli reported to the executive offices of the Church of the Seer at six a.m. The day began with meditation and hydration, followed by hot yoga and a good scrub. Ukweli had staff for everything. In addition to the yoga teacher, there was a stylist for his wardrobe and one for his hair and nails; there was a nutritionist; a chef; a kendo sensei; a jujutsu sensei; a speech coach; and a collection of young beauties for his bath and massage.

Even his midtown loft was decorated by a designer. He took all of his classes at Mercer online. Every public appearance was scripted, and he never appeared with so much as a hair out of place. The Church of the Seer even managed his social life and set up all his dates.

They eventually decided that Ava Sanusi would be his match. Her parents were Nigerian immigrants who were loyal to the Resistance. Ava was a nursing resident who considered her service to Ukweli an extension of her service to the Church. She was smart, beautiful, and agreeable to a fault.

AUGUST 23, 2042

Ukweli and Ava were out at No. 246, an Italian restaurant in Decatur, when they ran into Jackson and Kiera. This was Ukweli's first time seeing Kiera in person since she left London for college. Suddenly, his training went away, and he found himself unable to speak. Kiera got up from the table and ran to hug Ukweli. He hugged her back and his body forced his mind into a different space, on a different planet. His heart rate began to rise sharply. He was officially out of control. Ava kept her wits.

"Hello, I'm Ava. I don't believe we've met."

"I'm so sorry. I'm Kiera. I went to school with Ukweli in London."

"Oh, okay. It's so very nice to meet you. And who is this handsome fellow?"

Kiera blushed. "Yeah, that's my guy. Jackson, this is Ava."

Jackson stood. "Hello, Ava." He then turned to Ukweli and stuck out his hand. "Long time, brother."

"Too long." Ukweli shook Jackson's hand. *No headache,* he thought to himself.

"Hey, you guys should join us at our table. We can catch up."

"Aww, that's so sweet of you, thank you, but I think—"

"I insist. Have a seat." Kiera was still very bossy.

The couples sat and Ava heard stories about Islington and Highgate and football and kendo. Kiera told the table that she didn't think Ukweli could swim. Ukweli insisted that he could and offered Jackson condolences on the passing of his mom. Ava talked about becoming a nurse and shared some of her ER stories. They congratulated Ukweli on his football success and the near miss in the World Cup.

In all the talking, Jackson never mentioned the Company.

In all the talking, Ukweli never mentioned the Church of the Seer.

In all the talking, Ukweli tried not to stare at Kiera. He mostly stared off into space or looked down and played with his food. Kiera watched Ukweli. Jackson and Ava watched Kiera watch Ukweli.

After dinner, on the ride home, Ava addressed some issues.

"Okay, we need to talk about what happened in there."

"What? You didn't like your food?"

"Don't play, Ukweli. I'm talking about why you turned into a shy little schoolboy."

"You're being dramatic."

"Really I'm not though. You couldn't even look that girl in the face. Meanwhile, she never took her eyes off of you, not even once."

"So, you gone trip about this?"

"Absolutely not. I'm not dumb. I know my role. I also know that you've known her for years and you only met me recently. My point is, you have to learn to deal with seeing her. Especially since she's with Jackson Connaught. I've seen him in our briefs about the Company. He can be dangerous, so you can't afford to seem intimidated when you're around him, even if you're only intimidated because of who his girlfriend is."

"Listen. I'm not intimidated by him or her. It's just been a long time and I was a little caught off guard. No worries."

"Well, she might marry him so you need to start wrapping your mind around that."

"Hey, I'm fine. It's been years since I saw her or even spoke to her. I have no ambitions to pursue Kiera."

"And what if she has ambitions of pursuing you?"

"You just said that she's likely to marry Jackson soon. I hope she lives happily ever after."

"Yeah, okay. I just don't want to have to save you again. What would you do without me?"

"Hopefully we'll never know."

Ava couldn't hide her smile.

SEPTEMBER 2042

The Church of the Seer approached missions in waves. The first wave was reconnaissance and data collection. The second wave was the assault team. They were the warriors in the field who would execute the plans. The third wave was the cleaning agents. They discarded bodies and put out fires and returned the scene to a premission form.

The night of his first mission, Ukweli went out with Kelley Jack. They were both dressed in tactical gear, including body armor and face coverings. Ukweli was given a gun and a sword. He would get to choose his own later. Kelley had four guns and a sword but insisted she would only need her sword tonight.

Cross explained to Ukweli that he would have his own strike team, but he wanted his first mission to be with Kelley so he could see first-hand how a properly executed mission should look. The office received intel that a rogue torq assaulted two joggers on the BeltLine and had been spotted in Rose Circle Park. Ukweli and Kelley traveled by electric cycle—the Damon Hyperspace, equipped with artificial intelligence to provide real-time data, the bikes were fast, agile, and silent.

Ukweli and Kelley arrived and quietly parked the bikes.

"He's three hundred yards north. Stay low and move quickly. Let's go."

Ukweli followed Kelley in a crouched position. She walked with pace but did not seem hurried. As they got closer to the target, she told Ukweli to hold his position. She continued to walk quickly until suddenly she stood still. She drew her sword and lay on the grass on her back. Ukweli struggled to see in the dark through the face covering, but he watched closely as the situation grew more and more tense. He saw her, just lying there, and wondered if she needed help. Just as he was about to run to her, a large figure jumped out of the nearby tree and landed on the spot where Kelley was laying. She rolled away just in time and stood with her sword drawn, facing the torq.

He wore tattered clothing and his face was subtly disfigured.

He spoke. *"Watashitachi wa tome raremasen."*

Kelley calmly responded.

"Seigi wa kon'ya teikyo sa remasu."

The figure lunged toward Kelley and, with swift and decisive blows, she struck the torq six different times in six different places and stood silently as he fell to the ground. She reached for her communicator and simply spoke, "It's Done." Kelley turned to Ukweli and said, "Let's go." They walked back to the bikes with the same pace and the same urgency, then the two rode back to headquarters.

Kelley and Ukweli, or UK as the team now referred to him, would go on several missions like this one over the course of the next few months. Ukweli got to see, up close, the concepts of aggression and precision. Kelley was a professional killer. Ukweli greatly admired her and was equally afraid of her. She was as beautiful as any model on the planet, but Ukweli couldn't see past her swordplay.

Once, they went after a woman who the Church confirmed was purposely spreading AIDS in the midtown social scene. Kelley devastated her in one sword stroke without even parking her bike. Cleanup and ID swept the scene, and it was back to normal in less than one minute.

The same was true of child molesters, rapists, embezzlers, and any other criminal confirmed to be a rogue torq by the Church.

Oddly enough, if crimes were committed by citizens who weren't inhabited, the Church had no response. Cross made it clear that the Church of the Seer was at war exclusively with the Dark Reveal. It was not a peace-keeping organization, and it did not exist to replace local law enforcement. In fact, one of the reasons the Church was so adamant about leaving every scene undisturbed was to avoid any run-ins with local, state, or national law enforcement or military operatives. The wartime wing of the Church of the Seer worked silently in the shadows, undetected. The political wing, however, stayed front and center.

OCTOBER 2042

Kobe watched the video online. He observed as Remington Cross told the world about the rogue torq invasion and warned the citizens of the lasting effects of the Dark Reveal. His videos always included propaganda on the humanitarian work of the Resistance, which Kobe doubted they ever actually did and painted Cross and his merry men as Robin Hood figures who only sought the best for those less fortunate. They established themselves as the underdog fighting against the oppression and tyranny of the Company.

Kobe warned Ann about allowing Cross to dominate the information feeds and now the latest polls were showing that 60 percent of Americans and Asians were referring to the Movement as the Dark Reveal. Seventy percent in Europe.

He watched as the video changed from Cross's lecture on the work of the Church, to a video montage dedicated to the big justice and bigger heart displayed by his disciples, the most famous of which was now Ukweli.

Kobe couldn't help but be proud of Ukweli while understanding that he was a major threat to what had become his life's work. He knew that Ann wanted Ukweli dead and he expected she would succeed in her efforts at some point, but until then, he would just focus on his work and hope Ukweli would eventually learn to see things his way. He hadn't spoken to Ukweli in years. No surprise. What would he even say? It had taken this long for him to get used to his life without his children. In many ways, without his wife too. They worked together and lived together and did everything that a husband and wife are supposed to do together, except talk. They never talked. About anything, good or bad. They didn't talk about their work. They only exchanged notes. They didn't talk about Ukweli or Uzuri. They didn't talk about food or movies. They didn't talk before or after sex. They didn't talk about the Company or the Resistance. They didn't talk about Remington Cross or Ann Jefferson. They didn't talk about anything.

NOVEMBER 4, 2042

Jackson Connaught became the mayor of Atlanta. He won the race by thirty points. His slogan "Advance Atlanta" fit nicely with the agenda of the Company. His policies targeted the technology sector and made it possible for the Movement to have a greater impact on citizenship through schools and corporations. Atlanta became the new Silicon Valley, as the number of southern tech startups exploded.

Atlanta was selected to host the 2048 Olympic games and led the world in the number of new billionaires. The city was thriving. Even the Atlanta-based sports teams benefitted from the newfound wealth of the world's fastest-growing economy.

NOVEMBER 24, 2042

Ukweli sat at his kitchen table and allowed his eyes to gaze around the room. He and Ava were preparing to host some of her colleagues from the hospital for Thanksgiving dinner in a few days. She told him the apartment was nice enough and that it wasn't necessary to go all in on decorations. She said they could decorate for the December holiday season if he liked. It didn't make sense to Ukweli that the citizens of Earth still celebrated Christmas, given that it was a religious holiday, but they did. The shopping and eggnog and Santa Claus—almost all of it. They just didn't call it Christmas anymore. It was now mostly referred to as the December holiday season.

As Ukweli sat, visually exploring for some way to make his nice but banal apartment impressive, his doorbell rang. He got up and opened the door and was very surprised to see his old friend, Kiera.

"Hi, Ukweli. Close your mouth."

He closed his mouth. She walked in.

"Why, yes, Ms. First Lady, please do come in."

"Thank you, dear. How have you been?"

"I'm great, thanks. Congratulations on your family's success. Jackson is already making big news as mayor."

"He is doing just fine."

"I'm sure you're very proud."

"I am. We're getting married next month. We'll honeymoon in Paris."

"What brings you by?"

"Can't I come just to see an old friend?"

"Kiera."

"Do you and Ava have plans for Thanksgiving?"

"Yes. Why are you here?"

"Are you hosting Thanksgiving dinner here? Oh, I hope not."

"We are."

"I only mean that it's not very festive. So much gray and black and white. You should, at the very least, add a cornucopia to your centerpiece. We had a beautiful design last year. I'll have one of our guys bring it over."

"Thank you, that won't be necessary."

"Oh, don't worry. I insist. Anyway, I just stopped by to see how you were. You know, Jackson talks about you all the time. He really does respect you."

"Yeah, I'm sure he does."

"No, I mean it. While he absolutely believes that you're misguided and arrogant, he respects your sacrifice. Most people wouldn't have abandoned such a promising sporting career to pursue . . . well, whatever it is that you're pursuing with the Resistance. Of course, you may be an even bigger international star now. I see your face everywhere."

"One of the perks, I guess."

"Well, let me get going. You know, anytime you want to get together for coffee or something, just let me know."

"Please give my best to Mayor Connaught."

NOVEMBER 27, 2042

As the guests filed slowly into his apartment, Ukweli thought about Thanksgiving in Lagos Island. They didn't always celebrate major holidays—his parents were very often traveling during holiday seasons—but when they did, Mara went out of her way to make it special for Ukweli and Uzuri. He could remember the big, fat turkey being placed in front of his father for carving. The turkey was always much too large for a family of four, but it created elegance and a sense of plenty. Mara made sure the children got plenty of dessert choices. They were rarely allowed to eat sugary foods, but holidays provided opportunities for splurging. Sometimes they even got hand-held toys or new clothes on Thanksgiving when Mara knew they wouldn't be together as a family for Christmas.

Ukweli knew that he would never be able to recreate that kind of atmosphere in a Midtown apartment. Honestly, he didn't even want to. The object of the day, this particular Thanksgiving, was to impress Ava's friends and coworkers enough for them to reach a satisfactory level of jealousy. Ava wanted her friends to want what she has so much that they'd like her, but not so much that they'd not like her.

Ava wanted to be liked. Uzuri loved being not liked. Ukweli admired that quality in Uzuri and considered this to be a weakness in Ava.

In any case, Ukweli understood the importance of the day to Ava, so he went all out. The caterer prepared three types of meat, eight sides, and three desserts. The apartment was clean and well-lit. There were fall leaves and bronze art, and even a small pumpkin on the side table near the entrance. And, of course, the gaudy dining room table centerpiece, complete with a cornucopia overflowing with fresh vegetables. As much as he hated to admit it, Kiera was right. Of course, Ava had no idea this was Kiera's doing, and with any luck, she would never know.

As the guests arrived, some began to trigger Ukweli's senses. Kelley Jack trained his mental focus so that, by now, the headaches that always accompanied the arrival of a torq had turned to mild chills. So mild, in fact, that when Ukweli went on winter missions, he sometimes had trouble knowing whether he was sensing or just cold. While Kelley equipped him to minimize the effects of the sensing, she acknowledged that it could be a very useful skill in covert situations. Ukweli approached Ava to discuss their holiday guests.

"Hey, babe, can I speak with you for a moment?"

"Sure, is everything all right?"

"Of course. I hope you're pleased with everything so far."

"Ukweli, it's beautiful. The table looks great and the food smells really good. You went all out. Thank you for taking this seriously."

"I know it's a big day for you. I just want you to be happy."

"Oh, I am. This is perfect."

"Good. Hey, how many of your friends are torqs?"

"What?"

"Some of our guests are torqs. Do you happen to know how many you invited here?"

"I didn't know any of them were. It doesn't matter though. The Church is only at war with the rogues." Ukweli wished he hadn't said anything.

"You're right. I'm sorry. Please, go back to your friends. Let me know if I can do anything."

Ukweli spent that afternoon listening to stories about medical school and ER trauma and the possibility of new pandemics on the horizon. He wondered how any of them maintained their sanity while remaining in the medical industry, given their fear and pessimism concerning their opinions of the future survival odds of the human race.

The evening neared a close and, as the guests were making their way toward the exit, Ukweli encountered Dr. Emily Sierra and her husband Dave. They were both very complimentary of the meal and expressed gratitude for Ukweli's hospitality. He shook Dave's hand and, as he reached toward Emily, his vision went black and he heard a deep, sinister voice.

"We're gonna kill you. You're gonna die. We're gonna get you! Haha!"

Ukweli tried abruptly to snatch his hand away. When his vision returned, he was holding Dr. Sierra's hand as she and Ava asked him if he was okay. He slowly released her hand and apologized for his brief mental lapse. The couple complemented the décor, thanked Ukweli again, and walked out. Ava closed the door behind the last guests and turned to Ukweli.

"Geez, what was that about?"

"I told you, some of your friends are torqs."

"Who, Emily? She's the chief of medicine and one of the most renowned surgeons in the world."

"You've never wondered why or how? Ava, she's a torq and she's hosting a menacing demon. That's the first time I've ever had an interaction with one."

"Are you sure? She's never been anything but nice to me."

"I'm sure. You'll have to be careful when you're dealing with her."

Ukweli learned an important lesson that Thanksgiving afternoon. He was the face of an organization at war. When you're at war, you're at war until you win. The Dark Reveal doesn't rest. His experience with Dr. Emily Sierra provided a bitter dose of reality that served to harden his essence and strengthen his resolve. This wasn't football. This wasn't marketing and politics. He was at war.

Ukweli spent the rest of the winter focusing on training and completing as many missions as his body could handle. He and Marcus killed a torq in Indianapolis. He met Calvin to complete a mission in Jacksonville. He went to Palo Alto with Adam to dispatch a Stanford professor. All of these torqs had gone rogue. Usually, human hosts agree to inhabitation to possess special abilities, and it works for a while. The Church of the Seer was learning, however, that human minds and bodies weren't made for certain levels of understanding. It didn't seem to hurt a host to know about a thing.

But when human hosts were inhabited and experienced physical movements or mental epiphanies beyond their intended capabilities, this led to psychosis, panic, and fear that often manifested as violence or other aggressions. The reporter in the White House rose garden was right.

There is no free lunch.

DECEMBER 6, 2042

Ukweli sat in his living room and flipped through channels. He had gained a certain appreciation for American football as the rabid fan bases, particularly the fans who followed the southern collegiate teams, reminded him of the intensity of the crowds back in London. He figured that the reason the US men's soccer teams didn't have more of a presence on the international stage was because they devoted so much time, energy, and money to American football. Those guys were massive and fast, and he assumed a few of the local college players could've been outstanding soccer players if they had the training. Ava came in from the kitchen with a snack tray and drinks.

"What are you watching?"

"Nothing yet. The conference championship game kicks off at three-thirty."

"Are you really not gonna watch it?"

"Watch what, Ava?"

"The wedding, UK. Are you really not gonna watch the wedding?"

"Why would I waste a perfectly good Saturday afternoon watching a wedding?"

"You need closure. You need to watch that girl walk down the aisle and marry him."

"Look, I've told you before, I don't care what Kiera does. She can marry who she likes."

"I know what you've said. I also know that you still love her. You need to watch it so maybe you could actually move on."

"I have."

"Fine. If you have, then watch it with me. Show me that it's no big deal to you."

"Whatever. If I watch the wedding, will you leave me alone about it?"

"Yes."

"Forever?"

"Yes."

Ukweli changed the channel to news coverage of the pre-wedding red carpet ceremony.

"Wow, they're really treating this thing like it's the Oscars."

"It's the wedding of the century, UK. The Company's top man is off the market."

"I can't believe that she's marrying that clown, with everything she knows about him."

"Ha! So you do care!"

"No, I didn't say I cared, because I don't. I just don't see how she can associate with the Reveal."

"Wow. Pot, meet kettle. Your parents . . . hello?"

"They genuinely believe they're doing God's work. They're too invested to know better."

"Kiera probably thinks the same thing about you."

"Well, I'm right and she's wrong. I mean, we're right and they're wrong."

"Oh, okay."

Ukweli watched as the media coverage moved inside. The wedding took place in a resort on Lake Hartwell, a two-hour drive northeast on I-85 from Atlanta. The large, lakeside auditorium provided enough room for two thousand dignitaries, politicians, debutantes, athletes, actors, musicians, artists, and influencers to get a good look at the face of the Movement, and the world's most eligible bachelor, as he said his vows.

Ukweli took a deep breath as the screen grew dark and the cameras panned to follow a spotlight, which was now solely on Kiera. He watched as she walked, and thought of the first day he met her in the park in Islington. He chuckled as he remembered how determined she was to stop his shots, without success.

He watched and remembered.

Ava watched and judged.

She thought the dress was too gaudy, too much fabric for someone with Kiera's slim figure. She blamed the designer, who Ava said was making the wedding about herself and hadn't considered who Kiera really was. She thought the spotlight was too dramatic. It was their day, not just her day. Of course, she also watched Ukweli as he watched Kiera. She could see the agony behind his eyes and she doubted if he would ever actually be able to move on from her. More importantly, she was unsure if his feelings for Kiera would ever jeopardize a mission. Ava disagreed with Cross concerning Ukweli. Cross thought he was the perfect way to strike a blow to the Dark Reveal. Kelley and Ava thought it was risky, given the role his parents held in the Reveal and his affection for Kiera. Ava didn't doubt that Ukweli hated the Dark Reveal. She greatly doubted, however, his love for the Church.

Before the wedding was over, Ukweli changed the channel. He said it was almost noon and he didn't want to miss the gameday picks. She knew he didn't care about that.

"You know, Kelley said that you will have your own team next year."

"Yeah, that's what I've been told."

"You know who will be on your team?"

"No. They're only letting me pick a couple of my own guys, I think."

"Well, do you know who you're gonna pick?"

"I don't know. Definitely Adam and Paul. They've been training with Trent on the west coast so I know they'll be ready. Maybe Marcus or Calvin. They're strong. Charlotte could be helpful when we have missions in Europe or Africa."

"Well, you need to be prepared. You could be elevated at any time and it will look bad if you don't have your team ready."

"I'm prepared, okay? Let's eat. The wings are getting cold."

DECEMBER 7, 2042

Jackson stood at the edge of the viewing area near the top of the Eiffel Tower. He gave Kiera a big hug from behind, pulled her in close, and kissed her on the cheek.

"I'm so honored to be able to call you Mrs. Connaught."

"This is so beautiful, babe. This isn't my first time in Paris, but the lights seem to sparkle more since I'm here with you."

"I'm glad you're enjoying this. I know we haven't been able to spend much time together lately."

She turned to face him. "You're very busy. I get it. I'm proud of you."

"Thank you. You know, none of this would exist without you. You're my muse."

"I'm just glad that we're able to have this moment. No Company. No meetings. Just you and me in the most romantic city in the world."

"Just think, Kiera. One day, this will all be ours."

"Uhh, what will be ours, Jackson?"

"This. All of this. This entire world will be ours. We'll run things the way it was supposed to be run and then we'll hand it off to our children and we can finally rest."

"Okay, take a step back, Anakin."

"Don't you see it? We can have everything we've ever dreamed of. The Company has changed the world, Kiera. The entire world. All we have to do is claim what rightly belongs to us."

"So, let me get this straight. The moment I compliment you on taking a break from work, you immediately transition to a *Pinky-and-the-Brain* rant about taking over the world?"

"You're right. I'm sorry. I guess I got caught up in the emotions of the moment. I'm just so excited about our future together and I want you to know that you made it possible. You motivate me. You bring out my ambition."

"Well, this is our wedding celebration, so I want you to ambitiously romance me."

"My pleasure, Mrs. Connaught."

13

THE ALGORITHM

FEBRUARY 17, 2043

U K was preparing his gear for a new mission when Kelley approached him.

"Hey, I want you to know this will be your last time out with me."

"What's new?"

"Cross is giving you your own team next week. You made it. Congrats."

"Thanks, but let's not pop bottles too soon. I still have to survive tonight."

"We'll be in and out."

"I'm not sure, I haven't seen the whole recon report. Who exactly is the target?"

"Melissa Stanton."

"Yeah—I'm saying, what did she do?"

"Nothing."

"What do you mean, nothing?"

"I mean, she hasn't done anything. At least, not yet."

"I don't get it."

"The recon algorithm determined that she fits the profile of other rogue torqs."

"Profile? So, we're killing torqs now before they go rogue?"

"What do you care? You're a soldier at war, with a mission against an oppressive organization. Just follow the order. It's that simple."

"No, Kelley, it's not. If the algorithm decides our targets, then any torq can be a target."

"Look, if you're worried about your parents, they aren't on the list. Cross has promised never to touch them out of respect for you."

"I'm not worried about my parents, Kelley. Besides, they're influenced but they don't host."

"Haha . . . the girl isn't a torq either, UK. Nobody is gonna smoke your little girlfriend."

"I'm not concerned about Kiera. She married Jackson and I'm sure he's perfectly capable of protecting her."

"Then what's your problem?"

"Should we really be killing innocents?"

"They're torqs, remember? They're not innocent. They're the enemy. We're at war. Honestly, if you can't do this then I'm not sure you're ready for your own team."

"You know I am."

"Do I? What happens when you're leading your unit into a dangerous situation, and you have to choose between your ethics and your mission? Can the Church trust you to follow through? Can your team trust your leadership?"

"Yes."

"Show me."

Ukweli killed Melissa Stanton that night. It was quick and quiet. The only sound was the all-too-familiar shriek that accompanied the torq leaving her body and dissolving into the night air.

This was a mission, though, that Ukweli would never forget. Not only was it his last mission under Kelley, but it was the first mission dictated by the algorithm and the first torq Ukweli had ever seen show genuine fear. Ukweli knew Melissa Stanton had no idea why this was happening to her. Did she deserve this? The torqs who killed Uzuri deserved it. He wasn't so sure about Melissa Stanton.

(14)

KIERA MICHAELS CONNAUGHT

FEBRUARY 20, 2043

U kweli sat in a patio chair on his balcony overlooking the Atlanta cityscape. So many moving parts, so many people, most of whom had no idea the Church of the Seer had given itself the authority to exercise capital punishment on citizens based on nothing more than their *potential* to commit a crime. The thought made him uneasy.

Ukweli didn't drink, but he thought that tonight might be a good time to give it a shot. He opened the bottle of Hennessy one of Ava's coworkers brought for them at Thanksgiving, poured a small amount into a glass, grabbed a cigar from the small humidor on the counter, and returned to his seat on the balcony. Of course, he had no intention of smoking the cigar, but he felt like a deep-thinking adult with cognac and a cigar in his hand.

The air was crisp, but not as cold as he expected it to be this time of year. He sat and allowed his mind to wander.

He thought of the World Cup and how close they came to bringing an international title home to Nigeria. He thought of Ava and her strange coworkers. *How could she not know that she works with torqs?* He thought of Uzuri and Incursus and Melissa Stanton. He decided that it was not good that he was beginning to think of Melissa Stanton as an innocent, along with people who had been murdered.

He changed the image in his mind to Kobe Bryant playing soccer. Kobe Bryant died a few weeks after Ukweli was born, but Ukweli knew people called his father Kobe because of his super fandom. His father told him that Kobe Bryant played soccer growing up in Italy and Ukweli began to wonder if, perhaps, he might have had a future in the NBA had he grown up in the US. *This must be the Hennessy talking*, he thought. *Maybe I need a little more.*

He went back into the kitchen and poured a second glass of the smooth libation. As he recapped the bottle and placed it on the counter, he heard the key in the front door. Ava never came home during her shift, but maybe they were overstaffed. Not likely. Ukweli put down the glass and cigar, opened the middle drawer on the island, and grabbed the gun he kept stashed there. He kneeled in a defensive position behind the island and watched as Kiera walked through the front door.

"Good god, woman. What the hell?!"

"Well, nice to see you too."

"Nice to see—what?! Why are you out here sneaking around?"

"I didn't sneak. I used the key." She held up the key so he could see it.

"Dammit, Kiera, where the hell did you get a key?"

"Oh, Ukweli, people have keys to things. Don't let it trouble you."

"Give me that key, right now."

"Fine, but you already know I can get them so I'm not sure how this helps you." She gave him the key and he put it in his pocket.

"Kiera, what are you doing here?"

"I need to talk to you."

"I have a phone. Why are you here?"

"You don't answer your phone. Besides, I wanted to see you in person."

"Okay, let me try this again. Why are you here?"

"Why are you so stressed?"

"I'm not stressed."

"You're drinking on your balcony. Oh my, are you smoking? Ukweli Rahisi Aseyori! Your mother would be appalled."

"I'm not smoking. I'm just holding it while I think."

"Pour me a glass. I'll be on the balcony."

Ukweli reluctantly grabbed a glass from the cupboard and poured a small amount of cognac over three ice cubes and grabbed a bag of pretzels. He handed the bag to Kiera.

"You hungry?"

"I didn't ask for ice."

"Whatever. Drink your drink. Now, Mrs. Jackson Connaught, what brings you to my home this lovely winter evening?"

"I'm worried about Jackson."

"Worried? Why?"

"I've always known he was ambitious and competitive, but lately—I don't know—he's been talking about taking over the world and all kinds of craziness."

"Why are you surprised? Jackson was talking like that at Highgate."

"Yeah, but that was before, well, before now."

"Is something changing?"

"The Connaught family is opening a new hotel in New York in the spring. Jackson intends to go there and announce his candidacy for President."

"Really? He hasn't been mayor that long."

"Ukweli, with the Company behind him, he can do anything. He's going to run in 2048 and I'm concerned about what he'll do if he gets any real power."

"So, what do you expect me to do about it?"

"Nothing. I didn't come over for you to do anything about Jackson. I came over for me."

"For you?"

"Jackson is gone a lot, Ukweli. I mean *a lot*. We really don't spend much time together. I just wanted to sit and have a real conversation with another adult."

"You're the mayor's wife. You have people around you all the time you can talk to."

"I want to talk to you though." She got up, sat in Ukweli's lap, and put her right arm around his neck. She held her drink in her left hand.

"See, now you're doing entirely too much." She smelled like fresh soap and cocoa butter, and it was all he could do not to inhale her like a life-giving breath. He put his hands out to the side as if to prove he wasn't embracing the close contact. She started to softly caress the back of his neck.

"I'm not doing anything but sitting and drinking this watery liquor." She smiled from behind the glass.

"Kiera, you're married. And you know that Ava and I are living together. Why are you trying to complicate things?"

"You don't miss me? You don't miss us?"

"What do you mean, us? You've been with Jackson for years now, or have you forgotten?"

"You used to love me."

"So?"

"You knew I loved you."

"So what?"

"Why didn't you come for me?"

"Woman, this is pointless. What were you hoping to accomplish, coming here?"

"Fine." She calmly placed the glass on the small table beside the chair and placed her hands on his face. She leaned in toward him, and gently, but passionately, kissed him on his lips. She took a breath with her forehead resting softly against his and said, "If you want me to go, I'll go."

(15)

ASSEMBLED

MARCH 2043

U kweli was named captain of his unit in a ceremony at headquarters that contained little pomp and circumstance. His new armor was engraved and he received a handshake from Cross and a smile from Kelley. No one else was allowed to attend. Ukweli was given a digital report containing the names and locations of his team members. Adam and Paul were stationed in Carlsbad, just north of San Diego. Marcus was in Chicago and Calvin was in Miami. Charlotte was in Barcelona. Kei was in Sapporo. Each member of his newly formed unit would continue training and completing missions separately until the day came when two or more of them would be needed for larger, more complicated tasks.

Ukweli continued to combat train with Kelley, but he received and completed his own missions. Ukweli noticed he was exclusively given targets with evidence of violent activity. He didn't mind those missions. Each time, he imagined that this rogue torq was the one who invaded his home in

Lagos Island and murdered his sister. He rarely used his gun, even when it was more efficient. He told Cleanup it was because he could ensure silence, but he had actually grown to enjoy the feeling of his sword piercing flesh.

Ukweli hoped the Church had abandoned the algorithm and recentered its attacks exclusively on rogue torqs. He knew better. He was happy to work without the ethical conundrums, though. He figured Kelley would receive any missions that came from the algorithm and, if that were the case, he didn't worry. He knew she could kill anyone at any time, even bereft of a mission—so he was just glad she was on his side.

Ukweli spent the year completing missions and traveling to meet with the members of his unit to check the progress of their training. The Church kept him busy. He began to take a larger role in the politics of the organization, and appeared on screen with Remington Cross and Kelley Jack when the Church of the Seer made presentations to world leaders. Ukweli was in the media often, as the Church used his face in their advertising campaigns all over the world. Ukweli and Ava officially began dating, ending one media obsession and beginning another. He continued to live estranged from his parents. He loved them and wanted them to be well, but he didn't want to give Cross, or Kelley, a reason to question his loyalty.

MARCH 28, 2043

Ukweli and Ava married in the chapel at the executive offices of the Church of the Seer. Kelley officiated the ceremony, which was more like what would normally happen at a courthouse. "Do you?" "Yes." "Do you?" "Yes." "Congrats." Adam and Paul came to Atlanta for the wedding and served as Ukweli's best men. Hadley from the hospital came to be Ava's maid of honor. Ukweli met her at Thanksgiving and Ava talked about her sometimes, but Ukweli didn't really know her like that. Kobe and Mara were aware of the nuptials but did not attend.

Once the ceremony was completed and Kelley pronounced the couple married, Adam, Paul, and Hadley threw rice on Ava as Kelley pulled Ukweli to the side. "Cross wants to see you."

Remington Cross was in the building but did not attend the wedding. Ukweli spoke to Ava and asked politely to be excused. Ava understood. Ukweli left the chapel and walked down the hall to the office where Cross was waiting in the foyer.

"Congratulations, UK. That was a lovely ceremony. Just lovely."

"Was it? I blinked once so I'm afraid I missed it."

"Haha, Kelley is efficient at all things, I'm afraid. Please come in and have a seat."

Ukweli walked behind Cross into his office. He hadn't been there recently and Cross had made several changes. There were a lot more screens than he remembered.

"Wow. I see you've made some upgrades."

"UK, in our line of work you better have the best and the latest—which we do."

"We do. I'm appreciative."

"Look, as my wedding gift to you, I'm going to take care of your honeymoon."

"That's very generous, sir. You certainly don't have to—"

"No, I insist. You've become one of our best operatives, which is why I'm also giving you your next mission."

"Sir?"

"Your honeymoon is also your next mission. It's your most important mission yet. I'm sending you to Karin, in

East Africa. They have mountains and white sand beaches on the coast of the Gulf of Aden that rivals anything in California."

"Yes, sir."

"You'll receive your briefing on the plane. Your team will meet you in Karin."

"This is a full unit mission?"

"Your first one, I believe. In fact, I'm also sending Kelley along. She'll join your crew but you're calling the shots. This is your mission, not hers."

"Sir, is that a good idea? Kelley isn't exactly known for being a team player. Or someone who takes orders from anyone other than you."

"UK, this is a big job. I know you're up to it, but you will need to count on your team. Kelley will prove to be a tremendous asset."

"Whatever you think is best. Sir, If I'm allowed to ask, what exactly is the mission in Karin?"

"The mission isn't in Karin. You're going on your honeymoon in Karin."

"Sir? Then where is the mission?"

"Djibouti. Your flight leaves in six hours."

"What are we doing in Djibouti?"

"Your mission brief is on the plane. You're going to topple the government."

MARCH 29, 2043

Ukweli stood beside the airstair and watched as Adam, Paul, Kelley, and Ava boarded the jet. He quickly walked up the stairs and through the plane to the office to retrieve the mission brief. It included photos, maps, blueprints, and information about each member of the controlling family. Djibouti technically has a president and a representative government, but the same family has been in control of the executive branch for almost twenty years.

Ukweli's strike team had been charged with the removal of all members of the "Royal Family" from the government estate, including women and children. The youngest of the children in the compound, a twelve-year-old girl, was the same age as Ukweli when their home was invaded, and Uzuri was killed. The instructions in the brief were explicit. They were to return to Atlanta with the body of the Djiboutian president. There were to be no prisoners. There were to be no survivors.

Ukweli found it difficult to enjoy himself on his honeymoon. The team was stationed in a separate location to be sure that Ukweli and Ava had plenty of privacy. He just couldn't shake the fact that the Church was asking him, once again, to kill people, including women and children, who had no real stake in the war. They didn't even know they were in a war. How could this be ethical? Then again, what are ethics? Ukweli lived in a world that enjoyed so much freedom, people were free to decide their own ethics. Do ethics exist in the absence of a standard? Are all ethics subjective? If so, do ethics even exist? Kelley questioned if Ukweli was prepared to do what was necessary if he had to choose the mission over ethics. That should be an easy choice to make if ethics technically don't exist. Clearly, Kelley's ethics differed greatly from his own. That didn't mean he was right though. Just because his ethics were different doesn't mean they're better. Mission orders or not, he struggled with the idea. Seems his conscience was intact after all.

That night, Ava, realizing that his stress levels were high, gave him what she felt he needed. She gave him what she could. She gave him herself, and he was happy to have her.

He never really felt that Ava loved him. He always assumed she was with him out of love for and loyalty to the Church. It was a chore, or a job responsibility, for Ava to be his wife, he believed. A line on her future resume. She didn't trust him, he knew that. Not because she didn't think he was capable. She just always thought he was torn between the life he was living and the life he always imagined he would have. However, this night was different. For the first time since he met Ava, he felt like she genuinely cared for him. She expressed herself with her body in a language he could understand. He went to sleep that night a more confident soldier, with greater resolve and a clear purpose. Lead your team. Complete the mission.

16

THE MISSION

U kweli stood in the basement of the government compound in Djibouti. The president received credible intel
on a threat to his life, so the increased security measures and
alternate location made the mission tedious. His team was
perfect though. His team was precise. His team was ruthless. He was holding one end of a bag containing the body
of the assassinated president in his left hand and his semiautomatic pistol in his right. He signaled to Marcus to take
the bag and turned to make one final sweep before the extraction team arrived. As he walked down the hall, he met
Kelley coming out of a dark room. She stopped in front of
Ukweli and said, "All clear." She walked past him, and he
turned to follow when something caught his attention.

A noise. He stopped.

Kelley stopped and turned toward him.

Again. A noise. From the dark room.

"What is that?"

"Don't go in there."

"Kelley, what is that?"

"UK, we don't have time for this."

Ukweli grabbed the small light from his belt and walked into the dark room. There, on the floor beside the bodies of two adult women, was a baby. A whimpering baby. Kelley slowly walked into the room behind Ukweli.

"What the hell, Kelley?"

"I didn't want that on my conscience."

"There was no baby on the list in the report."

"Exactly, so let's go. The extraction team should be arriving now."

"You're suggesting we leave it here?"

"As opposed to what, UK? Taking it?"

"Dammit, Kelley. If we walk out of here knowing that kid is on the floor, how is it any different from putting a bullet in its head?"

"Listen, do you want to explain to Cross what you're doing with this kid?"

"I'm not leaving a baby here. It will know nothing of this war."

Paul came in on the comms with a firm whisper. "Extract is here. We're loading. Let's go!"

Ukweli picked up the baby from the floor and started following Kelley down the path to the extraction point. He was the last one on the chopper and Marcus closed the door behind him. The team sat quietly and stared at him as he settled, holding the child. He didn't speak to the team to address the child and the team didn't ask him any questions. He made a choice. He would take responsibility.

Ukweli had seen his team do things in the compound that would astonish the average citizen. The lives they had taken. And all in the name of what? He wasn't sure. He never sensed so he knew there wasn't a torq present. He wasn't sure how this mission fell under the paradigm of the creation of the Church of the Seer. He didn't know what he was fighting for anymore.

The team was already on the plane en route to the states when the news of the raid started to spread. The new president had already addressed the issue on social media, saying he would do everything in his power to find the people responsible and bring them to justice. Speaking French, he said the men and staff had been brutally murdered. He made no mention of the president's body, the shocking number of women and children who lay dead in the compound, or the baby asleep in Ava's arms.

Ukweli received a blink notification on his device. He went to the office on the plane and pressed the small button under the desk. The cabinet doors opened to reveal a screen and the details of a secure satellite connection. After a few seconds, the face of Remington Cross appeared on the screen.

"Good morning, Ukweli."

"Sir."

"Congratulations on a successful mission. President Luc has already begun to address the situation."

"Yes, sir. I heard."

"Now, as for the child."

"Yes, sir."

"You absolutely must destroy the child."

"Sir, what threat is the child to us?"

"If the Company discovers the child in our possession, they can prove our involvement. That would compromise everything we've built. Everything we've accomplished. We simply can't take that risk."

"What exactly have we built? You're asking me to kill a baby. What have we built? I don't even know why I was in Africa! What was that mission even for?"

"President Luc will return Djibouti to a free Muslim state.

The corrupt former president made billions in bed with the Company and forced the universal religion on a previously peaceful Muslim nation. We have restored choice and hope to a small portion of the world tonight."

"At what cost?"

"The sacrifice of a few will mean freedom for many. Freedom from the Company. Freedom to choose. That is why we fight, UK."

"Sir, the child . . ."

"Don't concern yourself, UK. The child is already dead."

Ukweli sat for a second and then leaped from his chair and rushed toward the main cabin. He found everyone sitting calmly, except Kelley.

"Where's Kelley?"

Ava spoke. "She went to feed the baby."

"Where?"

"The back bedroom, I think."

At that time, Kelley appeared from the back room. Her hands were empty.

"Kelley, what did you do?"

"What needed to be done."

"Kelley . . ."

"UK, it's done. It will always be done. It's over."

The team landed in Atlanta and quickly dispersed. The mission had taken a physical and mental toll on each member of the team, even Kelley. Ukweli recognized his own need for respite and encouraged his unit to suspend any training or missions for a few days. Mistakes and bad decisions were often the results of mental or physical exhaustion. Ukweli and Ava discussed options concerning the best way to spend a few days off, as the honeymoon turned out to have a dramatic conclusion. They both decided to just lock themselves in the apartment, turn off their phones, and rest.

Only Ukweli couldn't rest. His spirit was troubled. He was troubled by what Remington Cross and the Church of the Seer asked him to do. He was troubled by what he asked his team to do. He was troubled that they did it without hesitation. There were still many things about his new role that he didn't understand.

"I'm saying that I just don't get it, Ava."

"UK, we've been over this. It's not your responsibility to get it. It's your responsibility to do it."

"Look, I understand Cross is motivated by the personal freedom of choice. But, Ava, there wasn't a single torq there. Much less a rogue. I thought our war was against rogue torqs. And then, there's the algorithm. I guess we're at war now against even potential rogues? How can we fight for the personal freedom of choice, and then turn around and eliminate that choice?"

"UK, only the first tenant of the Church is to pursue rogue torqs. The other two instruct our actions to expose corruption and to pursue freedom. That's why we're here. That's what you signed up for."

"I know. But, babe, if everything is relative, then there is a fine line between corruption and desperation. Between duty and oppression."

"Do you not think corruption is wrong?"

"Of course I do. But who determines when a thing is corruption versus duty? How is Cross qualified to determine for every other person on the planet what's corrupt? He's a human, like me. What gives him the right to determine whether others should live or die? If every human is corruptible, how can any human produce an incorruptible standard?"

"The tenants of the Church are pure and not corruptible."

"Yes, but the men and women who interpret, apply, and execute those tenants are."

"UK, that's why Kelley's advice is the right advice."

"What?"

"You're a soldier at war. Don't think. Don't interpret. Just be a soldier. Complete your missions. You're literally the best in the world at what you do. Just do that. Focus. Win."

"Maybe you're right. I'm just afraid that if we don't have standards, then we're no better than the Reveal."

"All I know is that I never would've fallen in love with some demon-possessed phony like Jackson Connaught. My handsome Nigerian king is all man, top to bottom. Leader of the fiercest, most elite unit on the planet. The perfect combination of compassion and resolve."

"Aww . . . shucks. So, you're kinda feeling me, huh?"

"Captain Aseyori, I can tell you that my body has never experienced what it did in that tent in Karin. You're the only man that has ever made me make those sounds. If that's what comes along with being married to the leader of an international strike team, then sign me up for the next mission."

THE ELEVATION

17

APRIL 5, 2043

Jackson sat in the lobby of the new Connaught Hotel in Manhattan. He was flanked by several members of the media, hotel staff, and his personal entourage. One of the young men beside him stood and touched him on the shoulder.

"Your parents are here, sir."

"Thank you, Jansen."

Jackson stood and walked calmly to greet his parents.

"The hotel looks amazing, Dad. Congratulations on all of your success."

"I do it all for you guys, Jackson. I'm so proud of you. This is a great day for our entire legacy."

"Are you ready?"

"The question is, are you ready?"

Jackson, along with his parents and the group from the lobby walked into the large banquet room at the end of the northwest hallway. The room was dark, except for the moving, colored lights that helped create an atmosphere of excitement. Jackson walked behind his support group to the rear entrance of the stage. Kiera was already there.

"Hello, sweetie. Have you been here long?"

"Yes, but it's no trouble. I wanted to see for myself that everything was perfect. It's a big day for you."

"It's a big day for *us*, babe. I can't think of anyone else I would want on this journey with me. Except, of course, all these people who are on the journey with me." They chuckled.

A man wearing headphones and holding a clipboard came over to the couple and confirmed they were ready. He gave them a countdown from five and sent them onto the stage where Monica Earle, one of Atlanta's newest tech billionaires, was just finishing her introduction. Jackson and Kiera walked onto the stage to thunderous applause with their hands raised. After about a minute, Jackson stepped to the microphone with Kiera by his side.

"Thank you all for coming. I am truly humbled by this amazing turnout. I can honestly say I am motivated by your infectious energy. It is because of you that we have this opportunity today!

"First, please let me say thank you to my wonderful parents. How about this facility, huh? You can look around and just see the standard of excellence they live up to every single day. What a model the two of you have been for me my entire life. I can't thank you enough.

"Next, I want to say thank you to everyone who has supported me in my short time as mayor of the great city of Atlanta. We have accomplished so much, and I firmly believe that the best is yet to come! We're long from done. Atlanta is just getting started!

"I've saved the best for last. Please help me thank my wife, Kiera Michaels Connaught! Babe, you are the foundation of this entire movement. You are my sanity. You are my wisdom. You are my passion. You are my best friend. And I'm so proud to announce tonight, that in October, Kiera will become the mother of our first child!

"As you can see, it's a very exciting time for me and my growing family. So, without further delay, I am delighted to announce my candidacy in the 2048 election for President of the United States!"

APRIL 6, 2043

Ava sat up in bed as Ukweli returned from the kitchen with two steaming cups of water infused with tea bags with paper labels at the end of small strings that read "Akira Matcha."

"Mmm . . . thanks, love. Did you bring the honey?"

"Oh, yeah." He reached into the left pocket of his pajama pants and retrieved a small, bear-shaped bottle of honey and a teaspoon.

"You could just use the tray, you know."

"One less thing to wash."

"As if you wash dishes."

"One less thing for *you* to wash. I'm just considerate like that."

"So, what do you think of the growing Connaught family?"

"I think Jackson will actually make a good president. He's done a good job here."

"UK, you know what I'm talking about. Your girlfriend is expecting."

"First of all, please quit calling her my girlfriend. Kiera is happily married and so am I."

"So it didn't trigger anything in you when you heard she was pregnant?"

"No."

"Liar."

"I'm not lying, Mrs. Aseyori. Why do you think she affects me in any way?"

"Why didn't you tell me she came by?"

"When?"

"Right before Thanksgiving. And again in February."

"It wasn't a big deal. She was only here for a few minutes."

"Why was she here at all?"

"I don't know. She didn't really say."

"She didn't have to say. Everybody knows she's still in love with you."

"Still? I don't think she ever has been. She's been with Jackson since we were in high school, Ava."

"And yet she's making special trips into the city to see you for, evidently, no reason."

"Tell me what to say."

"I want you to say that you don't love her. And mean it. I want you to say that Kiera and your parents and your ethics won't stand in the way of a mission."

"Ava . . ."

"I want to know you are as committed to me as I am to you."

"Are you committed to me or to the Church? To Cross?"

"Do I have to choose? You're the face of the Church and the captain of a strike team. Being committed to you *is* being committed to the Church. And I am!"

"What if I'm not?"

"What?"

"Ava . . . I care for you and I'm glad you're in my life. I just have questions about the future of the Church. I'm here to avenge my sister. To fight rogue torqs. The Church is on a different path and I'm not sure if—"

"Shhh. UK, we all have doubts from time to time. As long as you rein it in and do your duty, in the end, it will work out."

Remington Cross sat at his desk, sipped coffee, and listened to what was a very disappointing conversation. He learned to love black coffee in the field. Sometimes, that was all they had for days. He spun around in his chair to face Kelley, who was sitting in her familiar spot on the edge of his desk.

"I told you. Ava was right. UK has become a risk."

"That is most unfortunate. He has so much potential. I'm almost sad for him, Kelley."

"How do you want me to handle it?"

"Do nothing. We'll have to wait. The timing must be right."

"What of his missions?"

"His motivation is violent rogues. Give him what he wants for now."

JUNE 2043

Kiera Michaels-Connaught sat in the examination room in the basement of the Connaught home where she awaited the arrival of her obstetrician. She hadn't requested home visits from her doctors, but Jackson didn't like her roaming the city. The only thing growing as quickly as the economy in Atlanta was the crime rate. Atlanta had become a city of the haves and the have-nots. As mayor, Jackson was aware of the considerable homeless population in the city. As the face of the Company, he was obsessed with the success of the elites. He had no intention of allowing some low-life street thug to have access to his wife or his child. He arranged for her to have everything she needed at home. In addition, he had a tracker installed on her phone, which she would conveniently leave at home when the cabin fever became unbearable. She, with the help of her assistant, would leave the house to go shopping or, from time to time, visit old friends.

Kiera didn't resent her life. She understood the motivations behind the Movement and she appreciated the life the Company provided. She didn't trust Ann and she didn't fully understand Jackson's fanatic loyalty to her, but she was having a child and he was running for office, so she didn't ask questions.

Jackson had always been arrogant, but Kiera recognized a growing darkness in him. His ambition, once budding in London, had grown and sprouted. She had seen him reading Darwin, Galton, and Grant and, for the first time, began to feel genuine concern about his political influences. Kiera knew Jackson was sharp enough to be a world leader. She began to fear he may be too ambitious to lead with compassion. She had previously heard him speak about Ukweli with respectful tones concerning his football ability and his loyalty to Uzuri. Lately, however, she only heard Ukweli's name as it was associated with Remington Cross and the Church of the Seer. Jackson began referring to Ukweli as a traitor and he believed that, were it not for Ukweli's parents and their position within the Company, Ukweli may already be dead.

Kiera carried a heavy load of regrets. She hadn't spoken to her mother since her wedding. Her parents never thought Jackson was right for her. They insisted he had abundant resources but no character, and advised her that it took more than wealth and attraction for a marriage to thrive.

She was now five years from possibly being First Lady of the United States and mere months away from being a mother. She simply could not afford to rethink her life choices. Hands on the wheel and foot on the gas, she needed to move forward.

She did, on occasion, allow herself to embrace the aggravation that came with the annoyance, also known as Nurse Ava Sanusi-Aseyori. Kiera knew Ava's true loyalty was to the Church, and Ukweli deserved to have real love in his life. Not that the fake skank would know that. How could she? Ava barely even knew Ukweli. She didn't know his heart or understand his passions. She figured Ava wasn't even that good of a nurse. *Folks probably dying left and right,* she thought.

Entering the summer months, Kiera's biggest regret, however, was spending the last half of her pregnancy in the heat. She vowed never again to conceive in the winter. Spring conception. Winter delivery. You live and learn.

JULY 2043

Ukweli spent the summer months on a mission binge. He ran about one solo mission a week, though it felt like every day. The targets that summer were aggressive and violent. The growing homeless population created a market for underground crime, and Atlanta saw a steep increase in human trafficking, prostitution, drug use, and violent crimes.

A relatively small elite class generated wealth on the sweat and creativity of a growing middle class pursuing the dream set out by the Company. Those who were not able to adapt, or were unwilling, were forced into the shadows, into the corners to fend for themselves. Eventually, a hierarchy developed amongst the shadow dwellers, and Ukweli found himself thrust into the turf wars fought between groups of the lacking. Rogue torqs felt at home in the slums and Ukweli made it his professional and personal mission to make each and every one of them pay for his pain.

Ukweli very rarely used his gun on missions. Remington Cross made it a tradition to issue a special, chrome and gold-plated G19 to soldiers when they were promoted to the rank of captain and assigned a team to lead, though most of the team members carried assault rifles. Cross used a G19 on his special missions when he was in the field, so he insisted that a truly elite marksman didn't need maximum firepower. Cross was trained to infiltrate facilities in the manner of John Wick, fierce and efficient hand-to-hand combat, one still shot, one kill shot. Maximum body count. Work thoroughly. Win completely.

Kelley Jack carried an AR-15.

Once, Ukweli walked into an ambush as he pursued a rogue torq into what looked to be an abandoned building. He crashed into the door only to find five additional torqs. Their demons all began to speak to him at once, clouding his ability to respond to their sudden movements. Ukweli took out his semiautomatic pistol and fired shots while slicing with his blade. One of the torqs was able to maneuver behind him and grabbed him, knocking him off balance. Ukweli hit the floor and spun quickly to recover. He replaced his sword and grabbed his Glock instead.

He fired with precision, with both hands, and listened, with relief, as the demons hissed and dissolved. He wasn't fully able to understand how he was ambushed or how the words of the demons broke his concentration. He knew he needed to continue to improve and that he still had a lot to learn about his enemy. Mostly, he knew that his carelessness could have catastrophic consequences if he allowed himself or one of his teammates to wander into a rogue torq ambush. He needed greater focus.

Ukweli didn't mind a body count, so long as they were the right bodies. The hiss of escaping symbionts began to sound like music. He no longer had dreams about football. He often found himself in the gym in the middle of the night, even the night of a mission, if his appetite for carnage wasn't satisfied. The atmosphere in the bowels of the city created an environment where violent psychopaths could thrive. Ukweli was starting to fit right in.

18

THE BIG PEACE

SEPTEMBER 1, 2043

The world changed following the institution of the Big Peace. After a series of debates between Alexander Scott and Kobe Aseyori, the Company and the Church of the Seer agreed to a treaty that would bring healing to the nations. The Church of the Seer agreed to suspend all missions, worldwide, for a period of six months during which time, the Company would invest billions in solutions to the problems of homelessness and violent crime sweeping the major cities of the world. It was a big political win for the Company, as they were poised and properly positioned to take full advantage of the world's desperate need for their resources.

Ukweli wasn't entirely sure why Remington Cross agreed to the treaty. It was well known that Cross was untrusting, and rumors circulated that he wanted to reorganize the Church. The three tenants wouldn't change, but there was speculation that some of the personnel would. This created paranoia within the ranks of the Church. Remington Cross was known to execute contemporaries that he didn't trust, even friendlies. No one wanted to be excommunicated from the Church of the Seer. That would certainly mean a death sentence.

Ukweli and Ava took advantage of the time off to travel. They spent some time in the Pacific Northwest and ate lots of seafood. They went to Barcelona and Berlin. They drank beer in Amsterdam and toured the tulip farms in Holland. Ukweli even took Ava to Lagos Island. The old Aseyori family estate had long been demolished. Ukweli had no plans to visit that site anyway.

The couple did, however, visit the field the Lagos city leaders named after Uzuri. Ukweli's parents created a $1 million endowment for the upkeep and evolution of the grounds and the developing stadium so that by the time of Ukweli and Ava's visit, it looked like a legitimate competitive ground. It reminded Ukweli of the smaller high school stadiums in Atlanta. He was proud.

They also ran into Samantha from school. She still had a pretty face, but she had gotten really fat. She had just had her second kid and hadn't lost the weight. Ukweli thought of how Uzuri would have had some not-so-nice words for her. He laughed at the thought of it, but he didn't say anything. *Fat people know they're fat*, he thought to himself.

They finished the trip by celebrating the December Holiday season in Islington with his parents. Kobe and Mara were charming and welcoming and treated Ava like a queen. Ukweli wasn't sure what type of reception he would get from them, but they seemed happy to see him. They treated the couple to a BBQ dinner. Kobe joked that he assumed that was how Ukweli ate these days. Ukweli took

Ava on a tour of London and showed her his old stomping grounds in Islington, at the Highgate School, and in Tottenham. He was very disappointed in himself that, in all of his reminiscing, his memories drew his mind to Kiera much too often. He had not been very successful in convincing Ava that he didn't love Kiera. Perhaps it would be more appropriate if he convinced himself first.

The young Aseyori couple traveled back to Atlanta to watch the peach drop on New Year's Eve. Ukweli and Ava's relationship was in a good place. They were learning what they needed to be to each other, and they were starting to appreciate the relationship as more than a business transaction. Neither would admit to falling in love, but both would acknowledge their growing friendship. In many ways, they needed each other. A genuine trust was beginning to unfold and it made them both uncomfortable.

JANUARY 2044

The world welcomed 2044 with a sense of anticipation that hadn't existed since the first year of the Manifestation. The Big Peace worked. Though some still had more than others, everyone had enough. The tremendous strides in nutritional technology made food shortages a thing of the past. Everyone ate. Everyone had clean water. The Company announced in January that it discovered a non-surgical, chemical-free cure for cancer and that it would soon be available to the population. The February announcement was that American and Chinese scientists created a chemical compound, to be deployed on the next space shuttle, that would lessen, eliminate, or possibly reverse the effects of global warming by reinforcing the depleted portions of the ozone layer.

The success of the Big Peace and the sharply rising popularity of the Company lessened the shock of the announcement that there would be no presidential election in 2044.

Ann Jefferson was proud to reveal that President James would serve an unprecedented third term and would be inaugurated again in 2045. The new slogan of the Company, Peace through Continuity, also ushered in several worldwide modifications.

With the Company working diligently to be sure that everyone on the planet had access to fresh food and clean water, they announced the StrongHealth tracking system. With one small microchip, the Company could control the distribution of resources to be sure everyone could get what they needed. The microchip was to be installed in the back of the neck, near the spine, so the Company could track the health and wellness of every member of the human species alive on the planet. This would streamline the allocation of resources and make the world a more efficient and equitable steward of resources. God would be so proud of his children! The StrongHealth system would also provide real-time data to physicians about their patient's heart health, circulation and blood pressure, oxygen and blood sugar levels, and a myriad of medical and mental health information.

FEBRUARY 29, 2044

Ann Jefferson announced to the world that the StrongHealth system and the implementation of the smart chip was a requirement for access to any and all Company resources, including food, water, and health care services moving forward.

MARCH 1, 2044

Remington Cross announced to all strike team members all over the world that they and members of their immediate family were strictly prohibited from receiving a smart chip and participating in the StrongHealth system. Cross

issued a series of strikes that targeted smart chip manufac-
turers and medical facility personnel. It was during this time
that the famed political terms made their triumphant return
to media. Remington Cross was considered a radical liberal
for his extreme pursuit of the protection of personal liberties.
The Company stressed that all freedom exists with bounda-
ries and that real freedom was possessed within the confines
of continuity. Peace through continuity. Freedom through
continuity. Continuity through unity. One Religion. One
America. One World. StrongHealth.

During the six months of the Big Peace, Remington Cross
collected data for a broad application of the algorithm. By
the time the missions began in full that spring, the algorithm
dictated more than 90 percent of targets.

For all of the ethical issues Ukweli had with the Church's
use of the algorithm to dictate targets, he considered the
StrongHealth system a greater threat and committed himself to the Church, to his missions, and to Ava.

(19)

THE BIG
PEACE ENDS

MARCH 17, 2044

T he Company responded to the Church's aggression with a strategic offensive of its own. Enhanced machines attacked agents and separatist civilians all over the world. It was official. The Company and the Church of the Seer were at war. For the first time, attempts were made to infiltrate the executive offices and the personal safety of Remington Cross was threatened. Cross increased his security and rotated a team of operatives with the ability to sense torqs. This was the first time Ukweli learned he wasn't the only soldier with sensing capabilities.

Even torqs with special abilities couldn't get through Cross's highly trained security detail, but witches like Ann Jefferson, and their ability to manifest, could appear as anyone at any moment. Only sensers could tell when witches were present. Witches were the only class of demon strong enough to inhabit a human host without consent and, as such, they posed a very real physical threat to Cross.

Of course, witches also ran the risk of being destroyed if their machine was killed while inhabited. Security was always on high alert for the presence of witches. One could find themselves doing battle with a fellow Church agent. Ukweli shuttered to think what would happen if a witch was ever able to inhabit Kelley Jack.

The Church received intel that torqs were gathering at abandoned sites in the city to prepare for an assault on the Church and its officers. Ukweli and other capable soldiers were sent to these sites to destroy any torqs they found there. Ukweli and the other rebels would have to rely on their skill and precision to do battle with torqs preparing for a fight. These were dangerous missions. It was why Ukweli joined the Church of the Seer in the first place. These were the battles he wanted to fight. This is how he soothed his soul. This is how he would avenge Uzuri. This is how he would convince Ava. This is how he would take control.

APRIL 2044

As Cleanup proceeded to ID the bodies of the hosts destroyed by the operatives in March, it was clear that the Company had been inhabiting and training kidnapped teens from the streets. During the Big Peace, the Company was forming an offensive from inhabited teens purchased from underworld traffickers. As it turns out, even the Big Peace was a lie.

The all-out war between the Company and the Church of the Seer went on throughout the spring and summer and into the fall. The Company focused on the executive office and other strategic locations around the world. The Church followed the algorithm and sent individual agents or units to destroy specific targets.

OCTOBER 12, 2044

Remington Cross summoned Ukweli to the executive offices for a face-to-face conference. Kelley was not at the meeting. Ukweli walked into Cross's office. Cross didn't stand.

"Hello, Captain. Please have a seat."

"I would rather stand."

"Suit yourself. I have a mission for you. Honestly, you really should sit."

"Yes, sir." He sat. "What is the mission?"

"UK, you are my best agent, which is why I'm approaching you with this mission."

"Thank you, sir."

"You should know that I understand the sensitive nature of this mission and you can choose to accept the mission or not."

"Sir?"

"What I'm asking you to do won't be easy. It will require a full commitment from both you and your team."

"What is the mission, sir?"

"We have to kill Jackson Connaught."

"I don't understand. Why the mayor?"

"Jackson is not just the face of the Dark Reveal, he's also been deciding the targets. It is Jackson who has launched the offensive against the Church. It is Jackson who has been constantly trying to get to me."

"That doesn't make sense. Are we sure of this?"

"The intel is credible. That's not the real issue though."

"Sir?"

"UK, you know when we run unit missions, we simply can't afford to leave survivors at a scene."

"Sir." Ukweli hung his head.

"I know it's hard to hear, but should you choose to take

this mission, you will have to kill both Jackson Connaught and his wife, Kiera."

"She's pregnant."

"We are aware."

"I can't do that. I can't believe you're asking me to do that. You know my history with her."

"You're my best agent and your unit is the best in the world at what you do. Surely you can understand why I want to see you lead this mission. We absolutely cannot allow him to ever become president. He will be nearly untouchable then. He's almost untouchable already."

"Sir, you gave me a choice concerning this mission. I must decline, respectfully."

"Captain Aseyori, this is the most important mission in the brief history of the Church of the Seer. This mission, this single mission, will dictate our movement for the next five years. I cannot trust it to anyone else."

"I cannot, sir."

"Please understand that whether you accept this mission or not, Jackson and Kiera Connaught, along with their unborn child, will die very soon."

"Sir, I beg you to reconsider. Either way, I cannot accept. I'm sorry."

"It's okay, UK. I understand. You're excused."

"Yes, sir."

"UK."

"Sir?"

"Take some time off. Perhaps we've been working you too hard. Even very motivated agents need rest."

"Yes, sir."

⓴

EXCOMMUNICATION

U kweli sat in his recliner with a tall glass of icy water waiting on his wings to arrive. He had become a fan of the Auburn Tigers after watching a clip of Bo Jackson playing American football. He thought to himself that Bo would likely have killed someone on the pitch and that he was probably the best athlete the planet ever produced.

He used a meal delivery service to order wings from a local strip club. As it turned out, they really did have the best wings even in a city known for its wings. He sat in his chair, excited for the big game against LSU, and waited anxiously for his food to arrive. Ava came out of the bedroom, dressed for work.

"Do you even watch soccer anymore?"

"I don't have much time to watch, but I keep up with my former mates in Tottenham."

"You know these people in Atlanta won't take kindly to you being an Auburn fan."

"What do they care? No one even knows."

"Yeah, I halfway expect you to go on your next mission wearing a number thirty-four jersey."

"Then people would really be afraid of me." Ava chuckled and left for work and Ukweli got up to use the restroom. He washed his hands and walked out of the bathroom and was surprised to see a slim figure standing in his apartment next to the front door. With a stunned expression, he managed to speak.

"Hope?"

"Come with me, now. We don't have much time."

"What's going on?"

"Now, Ukweli. We have to go, now."

Ukweli followed Hope out the front door and into the apartment across the hall. They watched the security feed on Ukweli's phone as three large men entered the apartment.

"Okay, let's move."

Hope led Ukweli to the staircase and the two of them moved down as quickly and as quietly as they could. They reached the bottom and got into a small, silver car in the alley.

"Can you please tell me what the hell is going on? Who were those men?"

"They're from the Company. They came to kill you."

"What?! My parents want me dead?"

"No, Ukweli. They don't."

"How do you know that? How did you know they were coming?"

"Your mother sent me."

"My mother? Where are you taking me."

"We're going to the airport. There's someone you need to hear from."

"To the airport? I don't have a bag. What about Ava?"

"Ava is in no danger and we can get whatever you need. For now, we need to get into the air."

The two traveled to the Dekalb-Peachtree airport just north of the city. There was a jet waiting.

"Get on. I'll fill you in after takeoff."

Ukweli walked up the few steps and stepped inside the aircraft. He turned the corner and saw a small man sitting in one of the seats. The man unbuckled his seat belt, stood, and held out his hand.

"Hello, Ukweli. I'm Alexander Scott."

"Yes, I know. You have a position in the Church."

"Ah, yes . . . Premiere of Religious Freedom. Such a prestigious title."

"Sure, okay. Wait . . . I'm confused. How do you know Hope?"

"Oh, I've known Hope for years. Your mother introduced us. Very wise woman, your mother."

Hope boarded and the plane began to taxi. Ukweli took a seat across from Alexander. Hope sat beside Ukweli.

"Hope, who exactly are you?"

"The less you know about me, the better. What I can tell you for sure, is that you are in danger."

"Why am I all of a sudden in this 'grave danger'? Is it because of the commercials?"

"I'm sure you know the Company has been watching you for a while. They've considered you a threat since you publicly joined the Church of the Seer."

"So what? I can handle myself. What's changed?"

"There are some things you don't understand."

"Then help me understand them."

Scott spoke up. "Ukweli, this war you're fighting. It's a one-sided war."

"That makes no sense. I fight for the Church of the Seer. I kill rogue torqs. We have a clear enemy."

"But do you know who that enemy is, Ukweli?"

"Yes. The enemy is the Dark Reveal. The Company. The group who killed my sister. The group who killed the pope."

"Ukweli, Kelley Jack killed Incursus."

"What? That's impossible. Why would Cross want to kill the pope?"

"Let's just say, there are times when the interests of the Company and the Church of the Seer . . . overlap."

"Overlap?"

"Ukweli, the Vatican has been bugged since Pope Gregory declined former President Rhett's offer to join the Movement. That's how they knew Incursus was radical. That's how they knew of his plan to give a very aggressive speech in Atlanta. That's why they instructed the Church to take him out."

"Instructed? Are you saying that Cross works for the Company?"

"Ann Jefferson, not Remington Cross, is the head of the Church of the Seer. It only exists as another means of control. The Company knew if they could organize the resistance themselves, they could control how it operates."

"That's impossible. Cross just asked me to kill Jackson Connaught. If Ann Jefferson is running the Church . . . why would the Company want Jackson dead."

"They don't. Jackson Connaught is in no danger. They were sending you into a trap."

"A trap?"

"They gave you an impossible option."

"They knew I would say no."

"Had you accepted the mission, you would've been ambushed and killed."

"So, either way . . ."

"They used your relationship with Kiera and your refusal to complete the mission as a reason to terminate you. You have officially been excommunicated from the Church of the Seer."

"But why would they send me into a trap? How would the Church benefit from my death?"

"You become a martyr. It's a play on the fear of the masses. It is further justification for the war."

"How does that benefit the Company then?"

"As long as the Company can make citizens feel unsafe because of the existence of the Church of the Seer, the people will always appreciate the presence of the Company and be open to inhabitation. By controlling the Resistance, the Reveal controls the people."

"So it was all a lie? It was a setup all along?"

"Yes, well, at least since you clicked the red button."

"And what about Ava?"

"She's an agent of the Church, UK."

"So, where are we going now? I doubt I'm safe anywhere in the world."

"There is still one place. Get some rest."

Ukweli settled in for the long flight and tried to allow his mind to wrap around the shocking news. He felt so many emotions and didn't know how to process this experience. Why would these people, who barely know him, risk so much to help him? How long had Mara been working against the Company? Were his parents in danger?

As the plane moved quickly over the Atlantic, his body was cast into dreamland, where he had an emotional experience with his sister. He saw her in a beautiful white dress, walking through a grassy meadow. He saw her safe and healthy. She seemed happy. He couldn't get to her or get her attention, and he finally realized that it would be cruel to interrupt the kind of bliss she achieved. She had earned her everlasting rest. He missed her, but she was better off.

A bit of minor turbulence shook Ukweli awake. He looked around and realized he was alone in the cabin. He looked out the window and thought of all of the turmoil and grief going on just below the clouds, knowing he would inevitably descend to face the new life waiting for him back on the ground. Hope appeared from behind a wall toward the rear of the plane.

"Wow, how long was I out?"

"A few hours . . . you must've really been exhausted. You'll need the rest, so I'm glad you got it."

"Hey, that was a pretty nice trick you played with the fortune cookie in London."

"Subliminal messaging . . . just had to get you in the restaurant."

"So, where are we going now?"

"Vatican City. There are some things you need to see. Plus, we will have support there. It's one of the last areas on earth not controlled by the Church or the Company."

"It won't take them long to know where we are."

"They're likely tracking us right now. They won't be far behind. We'll have to move quickly."

"What chance do we stand? The combined resources of the Company and the Church will certainly be formidable. They have agents all over the world, including my own unit, not to mention that the Company controls military power all over Asia and Europe."

"That's why we're here, UK. We believe there is a power that is greater than all of that."

21

ROME

The plane landed in Ciampino and the crew boarded a helicopter to travel the remaining twenty kilometers to Vatican City. They landed in the heliport where a sprinter van was waiting to take the crew to the Vatican. The group entered the mysterious Vatican City administrative building via a small tunnel under the rear of the property. They walked past a unit of Pontifical Gendarmerie and, eventually, through a small battalion of Pontifical Swiss Guard, adorned in kaleidoscopic regalia that reminded Ukweli of what a court jester might wear. They were guided through a series of hallways to a large board room with an enormous table. Ukweli walked into the room behind Alexander Scott and Hope and was surprised, and elated, to see his team—his full team—seated at the table. Adam, Paul, Marcus, Calvin, Charlotte, and Kei were all present and accounted for. When Ukweli walked into the room, Adam and Paul stood to greet him.

"What are you guys all doing here?"

Adam approached Ukweli and hugged him, "Hey, we've been watching your back since Highgate."

"Yeah," said Paul, "we figured there's no use in stopping now."

"Guys, I'm so glad to see you. I'm glad to see you all. But I can't ask you to do this."

"You didn't," Paul said.

Alexander Scott walked over to Ukweli, put his hand on his shoulder, and said, "Come with me." He led Ukweli around two corners and into a small office with a small desk and oddly shaped filing cabinets. After punching in a combination and clicking a small lever, the middle of five drawers opened. Scott reached into the drawer and pulled out a bright orange shipping envelope. He closed the drawer and directed Ukweli to sit in the chair beside the desk. He unwrapped the string around the clasp, opened the envelope, and took out a small piece of folded, yellow-lined paper. He unfolded the paper and handed it to Ukweli.

"What is this?"

"Can't you read it? I thought you spoke several languages."

"I do, but not Greek."

"UK, these are the handwritten, prepared notes for a speech to be given by the late Pope Incursus I at the Cathedral of Christ the King in Atlanta, Georgia. It's the last thing he ever wrote."

"The speech he never got to deliver."

"That is correct. Do you remember the final words Incursus spoke to me, just before he died that day?"

"Of course. You told Cross that Incursus said the Seer was the only way."

"UK, I was a mess that day. Can you imagine it? There in the back seat of the car, as the blood from the bullet wound soaked into his white robe. When he put his hands on my face and began to speak . . . well, let's just say I didn't interpret his words properly."

"What exactly did he say?"

"What I heard Incursus say that day was, 'The Seer *einai o monos tropos.*' I hadn't considered he spoke the entire phrase in Greek until I came back here and saw his speech notes. Please, flip to the back of the page and look at the final sentence."

Ukweli turned the yellow paper over and looked at the bottom of the page. There, written in Greek, were the words, *"Thysia einai o monos tropos."*

"What does this mean? *Thysia?*"

"UK, Incursus was indeed giving a very radical speech, at least for our current times. This word, *Thysia*, means sacrifice."

"So Incursus was telling you sacrifice was the only way? That doesn't make sense."

"But it does. People expect the devil to show up in a red suit with horns and a pitchfork. Consider the serpent in the garden and his question to Adam and Eve. 'Did God really say . . . ?' It wasn't his goal to get them to renounce God. He only wanted to blur the line. Incursus realized the demonic leadership of the Company has led the human race down a path toward subjectivity. The Holy Bible describes such times in the book of Judges when it says, 'In those days there was no king in Israel and everyone did what was right in his own eyes'. You see? The Company forced the world to destroy holy books under the guise of peace and love, but their plan all along was to encourage and escort us, willingly I might add, into an age of subjectivity . . . an age where no absolute standard exists."

"So you think the sacrifice Incursus was talking about somehow represents an absolute standard?"

"No. The sacrifice Incursus spoke of represents THE absolute standard. Incursus was making the case for Christ."

"Okay, I understand why a reemergence of the Jesus of the Bible would be bad news for the Company, but you said Kelley Jack assassinated Incursus. My team wiped out an entire household in Djibouti to reinstate Muslim leadership there. Why would Jesus be a threat to the Church of the Seer?"

"Remember, the Church of the Seer only exists to perpetrate a credible threat to the Company. If there is no Dark Reveal, there is no Church of the Seer."

"So a return to the absolute standard of Christ would be damaging for both the Company and the Church."

"Exactly. Neither party could afford such an inspirational and influential figure, such as Incursus, to encourage the world to seek Christ. That's where you come in."

"Me?"

"Of course. Your sister died because the Company didn't trust your mother to stick to the messaging. They brought you on board to keep a close eye on you, but they always suspected you weren't fully committed. Do you recall their attempts to talk you out of your ethics?"

"Constantly."

"The game plan was to keep you angry, focused on the bitterness of losing Uzuri, while building your appetite for revenge. As long as they could keep you frustrated, afraid, and full of hate, they could count on you being the face of the franchise."

"And how, exactly, would my exposure to Christ do anything to counter the hate I feel?"

"Jesus, as the absolute standard, led a ministry centered on love expressed in two ways, sacrifice and forgiveness. In fact, in one moment, as he was being murdered, he forgave and sacrificed himself for the people who were murdering him. Jesus taught that there is freedom in forgiveness, a direct contradiction to the messaging and methods of the Church of the Seer."

"I see why the Company and the Church wouldn't want this information to get out. Messaging is important and the masses can truly be fickle. What I don't understand are you and Hope. Why are you risking your lives to help me?"

"Honestly, UK, I'm not risking my life for you. I'm willing to die for this message. I would put my life on the line if it meant the world could see the Jesus Incursus was inviting them to. This has become my life's work."

"So why do you need me?"

"You said so yourself, it's all about messaging. You're one of the most popular people on the planet. People know you from your time as a Hotspur sensation. You can change the world, Ukweli. You can free these people from this counterfeit leadership."

"Alexander, I don't even know how much of this I believe. We studied the Bible when I was a child but that's been ages ago. Plus, where was Jesus when Uzuri was dying on the floor?"

"Uzuri was very brave and is doing better than us all. She has all of the answers we crave."

"C'mon, Alexander. What are we doing here?"

"UK, time is of the essence. In a matter of hours, this place will be crawling with agents—your former coworkers from the Church of the Seer. I wouldn't be surprised to see Kelley Jack handling this personally. You know we cannot let them get their hands on this message. Take some time. Talk to your team. Do what you must. As for me, I will defend this message. I'm counting on you. The world is counting on you."

Ukweli stood and walked toward the door and out into the hallway. What could he even tell his team? He knew the

Company was corrupt. He now knew the Church of the Seer was a front. Who could he trust? Alexander Scott was once employed by Remington Cross. Who's to say he wasn't in on the whole thing? As Ukweli rounded the corner to join his team in the large conference room, he heard a familiar voice.

"UK."

Ukweli turned around to see Alexander Scott standing in front of Kelley Jack. Alexander had his hands up and Kelley's automatic rifle pointed at his right temple.

"What are you doing?"

"We're here to put an end to this once and for all. Turn around and walk."

Ukweli walked past the conference room where he saw agents from the Church of the Seer standing over his team, still seated, binding their hands. He did not see Hope.

He followed Kelley's directions to the main lobby, out the front door to the gleaming white porch, and down the stairs onto the asphalt lot.

"Turn around," Kelley directed from behind Alexander. When Ukweli turned, he saw four strike teams spread out on the terrace, his team with their hands bound and forced to their knees at gunpoint, and the intimidating figure of Remington Cross standing at the top of the stairs.

"Hello, UK. Good to see you again."

"Cross. Maybe you can help me understand what's going on."

"I can. You're a traitor who has been excommunicated from the Church of the Seer. That is a crime punishable by death. We're just here to see to it that justice is served."

"You came across the ocean to see to it yourself? I must be pretty important."

"You have no idea. Where is the paper?"

"Paper?" Cross gave a signal with his hand and one of the soldiers took his pistol from the holster and fired a single shot into the back of Marcus's head. The suddenness of the escalation was startling, and Ukweli was admittedly shocked as he watched Marcus's body slump over. The blood began to stain the bright white concrete terrace.

"UK, you know I'm not here for games. Where is the paper?"

"I don't know what you're talking about!" The same soldier shot Calvin in the side of the head and his body fell on top of Marcus.

"Dammit, Cross! You're taking innocent lives!"

"Innocent? Are you serious? The things your team has done . . . and you claim innocence? Okay, I see we're not getting anywhere." He made a different hand gesture. The front door opened and Kobe and Mara walked out with Ava walking behind them. She held a gun to Kobe's back. She forced both Kobe and Mara to get on their knees with their hands behind their back.

"Seems like you could've called your wife to tell her you were leaving the country." Ava had a look of consternation on her face as she spoke, and Ukweli wondered if she actually felt he should've called.

"My wife . . . Ava, you'll pay for this."

"For what? Spending some quality time with the in-laws?" She chuckled. Cross stood next to Ava and looked down at Kobe and Mara.

"What's it gonna be, UK? Do I need to kill your parents in front of you to get what I came for?"

"Cross, don't do this!"

"Really? You're still not . . . okay, never mind." He signaled a final hand gesture and Jackson and Kiera Connaught came out the front door. Kiera, nine months pregnant, was uncomfortable and moved slowly. She was in obvious distress. "I guess you're gonna make me use my big gun."

"Ukweli Aseyori. It's crazy I had to come to Vatican City to run into you again." Jackson had a sinister countenance that distorted his face and gave Ukweli a chill. The darkness that was usually behind his eyes now created a shadow across his face.

"Mayor Connaught. I guess we just ran in two different circles."

"Funny thing though, UK. Was there a reason my wife was in *your* circle?" Jackson grabbed Kiera by the hair and forced her to her knees. Cross handed Jackson a pistol and he pointed it at Kiera's head.

"Jackson! This is madness! You'd kill your own wife to get to me?! You would kill your own child?!" Jackson laughed. "Of course not, fool. A Connaught child is a gift to the earth. But then. This bastard Kiera's about to deliver . . . well, it isn't exactly a Connaught child, is it, darling?" Kiera held her head down and began to cry. Ava began to laugh.

"Oh, no. Kiera . . ."

Cross walked to the bottom step. "Yeah, yeah, you guys are dysfunctional as hell. We get it. Look, I think you can see your time is up, UK. Either give me what I'm here for or your mom, your dad, your team—at least what's left of your team—and your slut of a baby mama can all die right here, right now. You have three seconds. One!"

"You win! Stop! You win!" Ukweli reached into his pocket and pulled out the yellow papers. Kelley Jack drew her sword and struck Alexander Scott on the back of the head with the handle. He fell to the ground, unconscious. She replaced her sword and grabbed the papers from

Ukweli's hand and took them to Remington Cross on the stairs. Ukweli stooped to check on Alexander then he stood.

"Okay, look, you got what you came for. Let them go."

"UK, I don't think you understand what it means to be excommunicated. You can't just walk away. You have to pay for all the pain and suffering you've caused. On my mark!"

"What?! Cross! You can't do this!" Ukweli moved toward the stairs. Kelley Jack drew her sword with her right hand and pointed it at Ukweli, with her rifle, also pointed at Ukweli, in her left hand. "Just take me!" Ukweli shouted.

"Fire."

At that moment, the ground began to shake violently. Remington Cross took a step back and grabbed a column for support. Several of the strike team members lost their balance and fell. Kelley Jack lost her balance for a moment but did not fall. The earthquake lasted ten seconds and subsided.

Cross repeated the order. "Fire!" As he spoke, large blocks of hail, the size of basketballs, began crashing to the earth. Kelley lunged to the ground to avoid being hit and lost her weapons. Ukweli quickly grabbed her sword and held it to her throat as the hail stopped.

"Cross! I'll kill her! Call it off!"

"Wars have casualties, UK! Fire!" Immediately a great wind began to blow and scattered large pieces of debris over the asphalt lot and onto the terrace. Everyone moved to dodge the broken branches of the courtyard trees as they fought to stay on their feet in the face of the strong wind. The wind continued. The sky grew dark.

Everything was quiet, though the wind continued, it didn't make a sound. Ukweli looked around, he could barely see in the darkness. As he stood, still holding the sword to Kelley's neck, he noticed nobody was moving. Everyone was frozen in time. The soldiers, having regained their balance, were pointing pistols at his family and his strike team. Jackson was pointing a pistol at Kiera. Remington Cross was raising his right hand and his mouth was open, frustrated at his inability to give a decisive fire order. Ukweli lowered the sword and held it in his hand at his side.

"What is this? Hello?"

"Ukweli." It sounded like a man speaking in a whispered tone.

"Hello?"

"Ukweli." Again, the whisper.

"Who's there?"

"Ukweli, *eimai ego, I Thysia, gia ton opolo amfivallete.*"

Ukweli lowered his head and stuck the point of the sword into the ground. He held the handle with his right hand and dropped his left knee to the ground with his face down as he kneeled.

"*Thysia, I . . .*"

"Stand up, Ukweli."

He stood but closed his eyes. "I'm not worthy to look into your face."

"Ukweli, open your eyes and see as the Father sees."

Ukweli slowly and hesitantly opened his eyes. The darkness was complete. Ukweli could see nothing. He could still feel the strong wind, yet there was still silence. No one moved.

"What is it you want me to see?"

"The young lady. You consider her your adversary." Ukweli looked in the direction of Kelley Jack. Instead of the tall, beautiful, ruthless warrior he had known, he saw a girl, perhaps five years old or less.

"Lord, she has slain more people than I am able to count,

many of them for no good reason. She took the life of an innocent child."

"She receives the Father's Grace. Who among you has the righteousness to determine a good reason? You, perhaps?"

"No, Lord."

"She has much work to do for the Kingdom. She will need your help and you will need hers."

"The Kingdom, Lord?"

"Ukweli, see beyond the darkness and through the wind. Observe your true enemy." Ukweli looked toward the steps. He saw an image of Remington Cross and the strike teams from the Church of the Seer. He saw Jackson Connaught. The image of Remington Cross morphed into a large, ghostly figure with bright red eyes and the face of a tormented soul. It had long red arms, if not tentacles, with long claws on the ends. The strike teams dissolved into similar creatures, but smaller and gray. Their faces were menacing as they screamed, though Ukweli couldn't hear them.

"What are they, Lord?"

"These are the beings who now have dominion here in your world. Men have willingly given them the authority they now possess to go back and forth and to Determine here. The man who existed on earth as Remington Cross died many years ago. This demon and his legions have manifested here and only represent a small portion of the true infestation."

"And what of Jackson?" As Ukweli spoke, the figure of Jackson Connaught morphed into a teenage boy being strangled and tormented by the clawed tentacles of one of the demonic beings.

"Jackson looked into the darkness and embraced it. He made his choice. The Father is love. The Father is just. His heart breaks for Jackson."

"How can we fight, Lord?"

"Though your enemy is great, you must have courage. You must persevere."

"How can we win, Lord?"

"By the might of the Lion and the sacrifice of the Lamb."

"Lord?"

"You must do all you can and trust the Lamb to do what you cannot."

"How will we know?"

"The Spirit will speak if you will hear. You are powerful in your weakness. You are loved in your flaws. I do not leave you as an orphan."

"Lord, if you leave, how will we win the day?"

"Allow me to introduce you to my friend, Michael."

In the midst of the darkness, a large, angelic being descended from the heavens in a blinding light. As he stood on the ground, his head was above the four stories of the Vatican administrative building. He alone seized the demonic beings, bound them, and deposited them into the center of the earth. In a moment, the angel disappeared, and the wind stopped. The darkness dissipated and the natural light returned to reveal Kelley and Ava on their knees while Adam, Paul, and Kei stood over them with weapons drawn. Charlotte wept over the bodies of Marcus and Calvin as Hope suddenly appeared to console her. Kobe and Mara were on their feet tending to Kiera. Alexander Scott rose to his feet and walked over to Ukweli.

"So . . . what did I miss?"

"A lot."

"Come. Our greatest enemies are approaching. We have much to do."

"I don't even know where to begin."

"When you feel lost, perhaps you can consult the engraving on your back."

"I don't have a tattoo."

"Many things have changed. It's quite poetic and very informative."

The words, inked across Ukweli's back in large print, read:

To rise in power

He who would be the Lion

Must first be the Lamb.

EPILOGUE

J ackson Connaught woke from a deep sleep. *That was a super crazy dream,* he thought to himself. He looked around and didn't recognize his surroundings. He was in what seemed like a hotel room, but there were no mirrors, no windows or doors, no television or radio. A small table lamp at the back of the nightstand provided the only light in the room. All of the walls were matte gray and the carpet was black. He sat on the edge of the bed, desperately trying to remember how he got there.

A voice came from a small speaker in the ceiling.

"Good morning, Mr. Mayor. I trust you are well rested."

"I'm fine, thanks. Where am I?"

"Elsai stin Kolasi. The Boss will see you soon."

"Kolasi? Wait, you mean—"

"Yes. The Boss will see you soon."

Jackson stood and tried to find a way out of the room to no avail. He turned back toward the bed and was startled by the sudden appearance of a woman. She sat on the edge of the bed.

"Come and sit. I'm sure you have questions."

"Who are you?"

"That's a relevant question, but probably not where I would've started."

"Okay, why am I in Hell?"

"Ah, yeah, that's more like it. Welcome! You're our first real guest to see the renovated facilities. I've been meaning to meet with you for a while. I'm glad we finally got around to it."

"Back to my first question. Who are you?"

"Of course. I'm Jennifer. I guess, technically, you could say that I'm the CEO. I'm not really into titles though."

"Am I really in Hell?"

"Yes."

"Why?"

"You signed up to join the team."

"When did I sign up for Hell?"

"Well, technically, you signed up for the Company's initial 18-U rollout in 2034. You're currently here because your contract expired."

"What does that even mean?"

"If a host dies while inhabited, the occupant returns here, and the contract expires."

"Wait, I'm dead! What happened?!"

"Yeah, you were ambushed at the Vatican. Big guy, made of light? Doesn't ring a bell?"

"No."

"Yeah, they never play fair. Anyway, so yeah, you lost. Big time. So, you're here with us."

"So, this is it? I'm in Hell forever?"

"See? I knew you would get around to it! The answer is yes . . . technically."

"You've been here two minutes and you've already said 'technically' three times."

"You have more to do. Once your assignment is complete, you'll come back here."

"What's my assignment?"

"Come with me. I'll give you the tour. We'll do a briefing. Then I can send you back to finish your work."

"Wait, if I'm dead, how can I go back?"

"Let's just say I have powerful friends and a real flair for the dramatic."

ACKNOWLEDGMENTS

As a follower of the person of Jesus and one who strives and fails to live up to the standard, I am eternally grateful for the symbol of the cross and the sacrifice it represents. I never dreamed of writing a novel series and had no intentions until this material was implanted in my spirit. I am thankful for the inspiration of the Spirit, and I hope that everyone enjoys reading this book as much as I have enjoyed writing it.

I grew up in a large immediate and extended family and it was important to my parents that my siblings and I embrace everything that came along with that reality. It has proven to be one of the most impactful aspects of my life. My mother, Dorothy, went to be with the Lord in 2018, but not before she shared with me her love for the Bible and answered all of my questions about Jesus and systematic theology. She taught in the public school system for thirty-three years. My parents never went to an integrated school, they graduated from high school before integration, and they both attended HBCUs, my mom attended Fort Valley State and my dad went to Morris Brown. However, they never let their experiences, growing up in Jim Crow South, stop them from being or doing or becoming. My mom was an avid reader and loved to learn new things. She meant a lot to a lot of people. She was able to listen and give godly advice without being tempted to share the news in the streets. She was a brilliant, highly educated woman, but had the mind and the common sense to make wise decisions about everyday life. She was regal and wouldn't have been out of place in an audience with the Queen of England, yet she was a great soul food cook and sang songs about bacon. She was truly one of a kind. I miss her. The world misses her.

My father, Larry, is the best man I know. He was born the ninth of ten siblings and was raised in the deep South, but he has prevailed against all odds to become a community leader. I have often described my siblings and myself as "aquarium sharks." You know, we're sharks deep down, but we've been fed on a schedule. My father is truly what I call an "ocean shark." He has worked for everything he has, and he has done it with integrity and has earned the respect of his peers. He served my mother in the last years of her life with consistency and tact. He made us feel rich even when we were poor. He is a leader of men.

My brother, Earl, my older sister, Monica, and my baby sister, Maya, are the calming consistency in what is sometimes a hectic existence. Honestly, I should go ahead and throw my cousin Avery in here too. We were raised like brothers. They're all educated. They're all great athletes and played sports in college: Earl, football at UGA; Monica, basketball at Kennesaw State/Emmanuel; Maya, basketball at Anderson/Emmanuel; and Avery, football at Gardner Webb—but most importantly, they're all good people. We genuinely love each other. We don't fight, honestly, we never have. We don't have to. Common sense and transparency rule the day. We do not skirt around issues. We have tough conversations and then we move on. I'm so thankful for you all.

My son, Cameron, has been through hell and high water and has come out on the other side. I'm so proud of you, man.

I'm thankful for my brother-in-law, Ed Geth. The guy is six feet nine, won a championship at UNC under Dean Smith, and spends most days following orders from his wife. My baby sister is a *lot* to handle. Well, he doesn't really handle her, but he manages to survive the days. That's worth a shout out. Good job, Rolly.

Thank you, Dr. Raegan Tuff, for—well—you've been my friend for twenty years so there's a lot in there. Thank you for all of it.

Thank you, Stephanie Hunczak Medina, for embracing nerd culture and for reading with me and encouraging me to write—and for drawing the cool rose on my dedication page.

Thank you, Kimberly Hodges Gibson, for making me laugh when I didn't feel like laughing.

Thank you, BJ, Trez, Bryce, Brady, Brielle, and Kal'El for being awesome and funny. Go get everything God has for you!

Thank you, Mrs. J and Mrs. King, for your support and encouragement. God knows what you're going through. You are not alone. Keep fighting!

Thank you to everyone who watches my Sunday school broadcast. I'm honored that you see me as a source of spiritual nourishment. Thank you to Pastor Ronnie Gantt and the Maple Spring Church family for trusting me with the platform.

Thank you to BookLogix for their thorough and thoughtful suggestions.

Thank you to everyone who reads this book. I hope it makes you laugh, and I hope it makes you think.

ABOUT THE AUTHOR

Kenya Fouch is a career educator and athletic administrator-turned-author. Kenya spent fifteen years in public education in a variety of areas: teaching math, history, economics, and physical education, in addition to serving as a high school football coach for thirteen years and an athletic administrator for seven. Kenya started his own academic advising brand, *15,* in 2019 and currently serves in the children's ministry and as a Sunday school teacher at his church.

Kenya is from Hartwell, Georgia, and attended Hart County High School before playing football at Georgia Tech and Furman, where he earned his bachelor's degree in sociology.

Kenya was heavily influenced by science-fiction during his childhood, gravitating toward *He-Man, Transformers, Batman,* and *Star Wars.* He also developed a love for video games, particularly fantasy, sports, and action titles.

Kenya's parents, Larry and Dorothy, raised his three siblings and him to value family over possessions, to pursue and apply education, to have a heart for the community, and to honor the God of the Bible.

Kenya has a son, Cameron, and the world's most adorable granddaughter, Hendrix.